About the

Dawn Dalton is a short-story author, novelist, screenwriter, and communications specialist. When she's not slaying fictional monsters, she's geeking out over fairy tales, Jack Bauer, sports cars, and things that go bump in the night. Dawn lives in Alberta, Canada, with her husband and their giant English Mastiff. Visit her online at *dawnius.com*.

Shari Green writes young adult and middle grade fiction. Her first novel for teens, *Following Chelsea*, was an Editor's Pick from Evernight Teen (2014). In her spare time, Shari can often be found wandering on the beach near her home on Vancouver Island, BC, Canada. Visit her online at *sharigreen.com*.

Denise Jaden's critically acclaimed young adult fiction titles include, *Losing Faith*, *Never Enough*, and *Foreign Exchange*. She loves talking with writing groups and students about her inspiration and fast-drafting process. Her non-fiction books for writers include, *Writing With A Heavy Heart* and *Fast Fiction*. Find out more at *denisejaden.com*.

Kitty Keswick adores writing short stories as much as novels. Kirkus named her short story *Death Becomes Her*, "Among the Standouts" (Spirited, Leap Books, 2012). She's written two young adult novels, *Freaksville* (Leap Books) and *Furry & Freaked*, which is slated for release late 2015. She's a professed Anglophile, and once spent a blissful month touring crumbling ruins in the UK. She loves twisting fairy tales with history, lives for make-believe, and even has a fairy door or two. Kitty resides fifteen miles inland from the sea with her hubby, stepson, and a very lucky black cat. Visit her blog at *kittykeswick.blogspot.com*.

Cady Vance is the author of *Bone Dry*, *Never Sleep*, and *The Madmen's City*. After growing up in Tennessee, she decided to embark on a grand adventure by packing up her bags and moving to NYC. Now, she studies for her PhD in the UK and dreams of seeing the universe. You can find her online at *cadyvance.com*.

Falling For Alice

Copyright © 2015
Dawn Dalton, Shari Green, Denise Jaden, Kitty Keswick, Cady Vance
All rights reserved.

Print Edition
ISBN-10: 0994283709
ISBN-13: 978-0-9942837-0-2

Published by Vine Leaves Press 2015
Melbourne, Vic, Australia | Athens, Attica, Greece

No parts of this publication may be reproduced, stored in a retrieval system, or transmitted in any form or by any means, electronic, mechanical, photocopying, recording, or otherwise, without the prior written permission of the copyright owner.

This book is sold subject to the condition that it shall not, by way of trade or otherwise, be lent, resold, hired out, or otherwise circulated without the publisher's prior consent in any form of binding or cover other than that in which it is published and without a similar condition including this condition being imposed on the subsequent purchaser. Under no circumstances may any part of this book be photocopied for resale.

This is a work of fiction. Any similarity between the characters and situations within its pages and places or persons, living or dead, is unintentional and coincidental.

National Library of Australia Cataloguing-in-Publication entry
Creator: Dalton, Dawn, author.
Title: Falling for Alice / Dawn Dalton, Shari Green, Denise Jaden, Kitty Keswick, Cady Vance ; Jessica Bell (editor).
ISBN: 9780994283702 (paperback)
Target Audience: For young adults.
Subjects: Alice (Fictitious character : Carroll) Carroll, Lewis,
1832-1898--Characters--Alice.
Short stories.
Fantasy fiction.
Other Creators/Contributors: Green, Shari, author. Jaden, Denise, author. Keswick, Kitty, author. Vance, Cady, author. Bell, Jessica, editor.
Dewey Number: A823.008766

Cover art: © Larissa Kulik
Cover design: Jessica Bell
Interior design: Amie McCracken
Website: www.fallingforaliceanthology.com

FALLING for ALICE

DAWN DALTON, SHARI GREEN, DENISE JADEN, KITTY KESWICK, CADY VANCE

Vine Leaves Press
Melbourne, Vic, Australia | Athens, Attica, Greece

♥

With her wide-eyed innocence, curious curiosity, and famous sense of adventure, Lewis Carroll's Alice has inspired generations of dreamers—readers of all ages who, like Alice, long for their own Wonderland.

Kitty Keswick is also a dreamer, and it is her sense of adventure and curiosity that brought us together and inspired this anthology. Each of us has interpreted Alice in our own way, but there is one constant: we have all fallen for Alice all over again.

Thank you, Kitty, for leading us down the Rabbit Hole to begin this magical journey.

And, special thanks to our publisher, Jessica Bell, at Vine Leaves Press, who not only designed FALLING FOR ALICE's perfect cover, but also gave our Alice a place to dream.

♥

Contents

Brief History of *Alice in Wonderland* 8
Drunk 11
Alice at Woodstock 37
White Rabbit Rx 59
Wormhole to Wonderland 79
Wonder in the Stars 106

Brief History of *Alice in Wonderland*

by Kitty Keswick

In 1865, Charles Lutwidge Dodgson (1832-1898) had his manuscript *Alice's Adventures in Wonderland* published by MacMillan (London, England). One hundred and fifty years later, we still celebrate that adventure.

The nebbish English mathematician wrote of a fantastical world, riddled with nonsense and exploits that even now captures the hearts of contemporary readers. During one of his picnic boat rides with the Dean of Christ Church's three daughters—Ina, Edith, and Alice Liddell—Dodgson made up a short tale about a young girl named Alice and her adventure. The middle daughter, Alice Liddell encouraged Dodgson to write his tale down, which he did. Originally, he had titled it *Alice's Adventures Under Ground*. He produced a homemade book complete with illustrations and presented it to Alice Liddell as a Christmas present. He later expanded it into the tale we know and love.

Brief History of Alice in Wonderland

Dodgson published it under the pen name Lewis Carroll, which he first used for a short romantic poem entitled *Solitude* that was printed in *The Train* in 1856. What started out as a tale told in a boat to three young girls, blossomed into the fantasy tale that has inspired spin-off novels, movies, fashion, merchandise and so much more.

Alice lives on in our world.

Down the rabbit hole has become a common phrase in English. Many other wonderful Alice-inspired phrases, such as *off with their heads* and *we're all mad here*, are part of our everyday lives and we might not even stop to notice their effect.

During his time, Carroll met with critics—as most authors have come to understand, criticism and the business of public art go hand in hand. Many dismiss his work as childish nonsense. But, you see, it's the story's nonsense that makes it so endearing. With clever unsolvable questions such as, *Why is a raven like a writing desk?* and wonderful advice given by a hooka-smoking caterpillar to the Cheshire cat, Alice's world sticks with us long after we leave Wonderland. Carroll's words hold a treasure trove of wisdom ingeniously cloaked within the pages of his tale. Many life lessons can be lifted from Alice and her adventures.

Here are some popular quotes from *Alice in Wonderland*. We'd love to hear your favourites.

"I can't go back to yesterday; I was a different person then."

"If everybody minded their own business—the world would go round a deal faster than it does."

"Begin at the beginning—and then go on until you come to the end, then stop."

Falling for Alice

New Alice. New Wonderland. New stories to love.

Our short stories in *Falling for Alice* are written as homage to Carroll's creativity and exploratory spirit. Everyone benefits from a bit of make-believe and nonsense every now and then, right? We've been creative with Alice and her world, and added a hefty dose of our own imaginations.

This is not your mother's Alice.

Happy 150th birthday, Alice, my dear! You look wonderful for your age.

Drunk

by Dawn Dalton

Scratch.
    Scratchie, scratch.

Alice digs her pencil into the notebook as though carving a warning, the small, stick letters darkening with each pass of the dulled lead. The words look almost three-dimensional, angry, demonic even.

Scratch.
Scratchie, scratch.
One, two, he's coming for you.

Alice shakes her head and her hair tumbles forward in tangled strands of black, ends split and frayed, greasy. Her thumb is raw and sore. A small callous has formed on the inside of her bony middle finger.

Three, four, better shut the—
Crack.

The pencil tip snaps.

Alice shifts her gaze from the notepad to the door. Her small

flashlight casts the room into shades of grey, the shiny brass handle now muted, dull against the wood. Elongated shadows emerge from the floor cracks, arms and legs, whiskers and paws closing in, threatening to snuff
her
out.

She pushes her back into the corner, curling against the wall, naked legs bent toward her chest. A tattered t-shirt, pulled down to mid-calf, stretches across her thighs and knees. The floor is cool beneath her panties.

Alice looks down at the page, tracing the bold letters with her fingertip, digging her nail into the thin paper.

Scratch.

Scratchie, scratch.

The voice threads itself into her brain, twisting its way down her dry throat, pushing against bile that's been lodged there for hours, days, a lifetime. She can't get rid of it, can't swallow the feeling that at any moment, someone, something, will burst through her closet door.

Shut up. Shut up, SHUT the HELL up.

Five, six, grab the crucifix.

Alice chews on her thumb. Her teeth grate against the nail bed, stripping black polish, exposing weathered lines and crevices from years of biting.

Scratch. Scratchie, scratch.

Scraaape.

Alice's upper teeth cut into the nail until it throbs. She bites and then sucks away the sting, sticks her whole thumb in her mouth. The moist heat of her saliva cools the pain.

Seven, eight, better stay up late.

On the other side of the door, the second hand of an antique pocket watch moves in hypnotic rhythm.

Tick.

Drunk

Tock.
One second. Two.
He's coming for you.
Alice squeezes her eyes shut. She starts at the beginning. *One …* Her chest constricts, heart racing so fast she's afraid it will just—
STOP.
Alice flicks open a switchblade and begins scratching at her notebook with the sharp edge of the knife, lightly, and then harder as though the letters can be scraped clean. She digs the tip of the knife into the center of the page.
Riiiip.
Alice inhales, holds her breath. She pushes open the door and peers into the blinding light. Her heart skips a full beat.
He's there.
The White Rabbit.
Leering. Mocking.
He's coming for you.
Scrambling forward, Alice grabs the stuffed animal, bunches its stained and mottled fur in her hand and draws it to her chest, willing it to somehow quench her thirst.
The rabbit remains limp.
Dead. *Undead.*
And instead of satiating her need, it is sucking her dry.
Shadows furl around it like a protective shield. A single tear crawls down Alice's cheek as she plunges the blade deep into the animal's heart.

♥

Alice's eyes snap open at the sound of a voice, a morning birdsong close, too close. Right outside her door.
Her mother knocks. "A?"

Falling for Alice

Alice knows she should answer, but a response lodges in her throat. She curls up on her mattress and pulls the blanket up over her head to block the light, the sound, the memories. Her body feels like lead. Not brittle like her broken pencil, heavy like bricks and boulders. Unmoving.
Dead.
Not dead. Almost dead.
Another knock. "Alice, honey? It's getting late. I can't drive you to school if you miss the bus." A pause. Then, "Alice?"
The door handle turns, creaks. Energy shifts as her mother steps into the room. Her floral perfume masks the musky afterscent of dried blood, salty tears.
"Couldn't sleep," Alice croaks, as though a tiny frog bounces from her esophagus to her tongue, digging in its sharp claws. She pokes one arm out from under the woolen blanket. "I'm awake."
Soft footsteps patter on the plush carpet, punctuated by coughs and spurts of motion. Alice wonders if she remembered to shut the closet door, or if her mother will find the notebook and leftover shards of pencil on the floor.
Or the knife lodged in the stuffed rabbit's heart.
Her stomach clenches as familiar GUILT tiptoes across her chest.
"Another nightmare?" her mother says.
Alice licks her cracked lips, moistens them with CONCERN'S sweet tang.
"Or, is there a monster in your closet?"
There's a smile in the question, but the intended joke hits close, way too close, and Alice shudders, almost light headed with renewed FEAR. How can she explain that *she* is the monster?
The cravings are stronger now, out of control. How much longer can she hide this thirst, this *need*?
"When you were a kid, we chased those bad guys away with

Drunk

Windex," her mother says, and Alice licks up the words like candy. "Remember?"

Her shoulders sag. "The bad guys seem worse when you're not a kid anymore," she whispers.

"They're no match for the strong, beautiful young woman you've become," her mother says and rubs her arm, spreading warmth even through the blanket.

Beautiful monster?

CONFIDENCE. BELIEF. UNCONDITIONAL LOVE. Alice absorbs the emotions through her mother's touch, each feeling pulsing through her veins and easing the desperate thirst that burns through muscle and flesh like acid. She pushes away SELF-DOUBT, SHOCK, SADNESS; allows her mother's LOVE to fill her.

Don't—
Drink too much.

"Up and at 'em," her mother finally says. "The bus waits for no one, not even my girl."

Alice longs to pull her mother into her, stuff her into her soul, and carry her everywhere, to allow this LOVE to flow through her, give her life, make her forget.

Instead, she waits for her to leave and go somewhere Alice can't touch her or hurt her.

Drain her.

When it's safe, Alice shoves the blankets away and sits upright, squinting as morning sunlight shines through the lace curtains and stings her eyes. She swings her legs around so that her feet hang above the floor, and curls her toes into the shaggy area rug, tracing a shape with her left foot. The heart imprint stares back at her, smirking. Alice rubs her foot back and forth until the image fades.

She weaves her way through the furniture—an armoire, bedside tables, the Victorian dollhouse—given to her by her father two days before he walked away from her, from her mother, from the life he claimed to LOVE.

Alice's tongue turns to ash.

She peers through one of the small dollhouse windows. Tucked under the floral blankets on the master bed lies a picture of her father, the stuffed White Rabbit under his arm, sucking up his LOVE. It is almost *alive* with it.

The edges of the photograph curl upward, proof it's still there, hasn't been stolen, hasn't gone … missing. Walked away like it never existed, like *she* never existed.

Leaving her empty and thirsty.

A cool breeze flutters the sheer curtains surrounding Alice's giant canopy bed. Sunbeams reflect off the hardwood floor, bouncing off the mirror at her dressing table, and like an arrow, point toward the closet. It's open enough for her to see the menacing shadows of not-so-normal swirling within.

She crosses the room and slams the door shut, pushing it tight. Her entire body trembles.

But something calls to her from within. She eases open the door until light floods the cramped space. White stuffing covers the hardwood like a cotton field after a windstorm. The rabbit lies on the center of the floor, blade protruding from its small chest.

Alice squeaks out a sob.

She yanks the knife from the rabbit's soft fur and gathers him into her arms, collecting the shredded pieces of batting scattered across the floor. Pushing them one by one into his chest, until it spills over, until it overflows with life and LOVE.

It's not enough. It's never enough.

Her mouth is parched; she is desperate for more.

Alice drags the rabbit to her dressing table, withdraws a nee-

Drunk

dle and red thread, and begins stitching the fur in careful criss-crosses, pulling the string tight, and knotting it over and over and over until it is a thick scar of red.

The scars are everywhere, a familiar labyrinth of crudely stitched lines.

Alice knows not even this will keep the darkness contained.

♥

Alice shoulders her way to the back of the bus, bumping into DISGUST, PRIDE. Now, ENVY.

The blonde girl pressing against her back faces a brunette cuddled next to her boyfriend. Alice knows them, their stories—the love triangle that feeds their emotions, and her skin itches as the first anxious twinges of JEALOUSY seep into her pores.

She steps forward, breaking the connection with the blonde, and settles into a seat two rows from the back. Inserting her headphones to block the white noise of chatter, she stares out the window, watching the houses, trees, and pedestrians pass in a blur.

"Can I sit here?"

Alice doesn't look up to acknowledge the female voice. She hoists her backpack onto the empty seat. The Rabbit's stained fur pokes through the top.

One, two. He's coming for you.

Alice doesn't look up, but as the girl stomps away, white-hot ANGER spikes the air.

Go ahead, call me a bitch, a snob.

A freak.

Alice raises the volume on her iPod so she can't hear the insults, knowing it will echo through the bus, become a continuous chant in her mind until she has no choice but to hunt, feed, to satisfy her thirst.

Marilyn Manson screams in her ear about vampires.

Falling for Alice

Alice shuffles to the next song.

♥

Third period. Math. Alice struggles with equations, the formulas, the rising ANXIETY gurgling along the back of her throat.

Mrs. Kratky writes another question on the chalkboard with long, skinny fingers, fingers so pale they merge with the chalk. The scrape of her nail against the surface echoes in Alice's head.

Scratch.
Scratchie. Scratch.
Scrrrrraaaape.

Alice opens a tube of Chapstick and applies a generous layer. Too late, the skin flakes off and sprinkles like dandruff down the front of her t-shirt, across her flat chest. She flicks it clean with her fingers, noticing the veins on the top of her right hand. Thick and bulky, like they want to pop right out of her skin. They pulsate with blood.

Alice's throat constricts.

Mrs. Kratky's voice snaps. "Alice? Do you know the answer?"

"I wasn't listening."

The teacher tsks under her breath, points to another student. "Matt?"

Alice knows she won't have a response. The class doesn't understand math, doesn't *like* math. RESENTMENT, BITTERNESS, BOREDOM, an unwieldy bouquet of negative energy fills the sparse room. Suffocating. Nauseating. She is desperate to leave.

The pocket watch in Alice's backpack clicks as the second hand moves.

Tick.
Tock.

She grabs her pencil, flips open her notebook, and transfers

Drunk

the equation from the blackboard to paper.
Scratchie, scr—
Shut up. Shut up. Shut the FUCK up.
At the front of the class, Mrs. Kratky explains the formula aloud in a high pitch, almost squeal. Yet her words muffle under the *scrape, scrape, scrreeech* of chalk. A shiver runs along Alice's spine.

She reaches back and rubs her neck. Her hair is a sweaty, sticky, mass, matted to the base of her skull. When she pulls away her hand, a clump of hair sticks to her palm.

Manicured fingers clutch her forearm. "Alice, are you feeling okay? You're so ... pale."

Alice stares at the brunette, stares right *through* her, struggling to place her, figure out who she is. The bus, school, she's in a classroom. Everyone's looking at her. Pointing. Questioning. Judging.

Stop staring at me.
Stop touching me.
The words don't come out. Genuine CONCERN, WORRY, feelings she can't pin point, radiate from the girl. Alice drinks, slurps, sucks it all in.

Don't let go. Don't.
Let go.
Alice tilts her head back. Her skin tingles and prickles. She wants to break the connection, knows she *must*, but this adrenaline satiates her thirst. Her need.

Heat flushes to her cheeks, her forehead, creeps along her neck, spreading throughout her skin. Overwhelming her with pleasure, and something more, something undefined.

What is *this Wonderland?*

"I'm ... fine," Alice says. And it's true. She wants to stand on her desk and shout out at the ceiling. Sing. Dance. Everything at once.

Falling for Alice

The brunette's cell phone chirps. She looks up at Alice with SHOCK, CONFUSION, something akin to FEAR. Now *her* face has paled, skin the colour of rice paper.

The pitter-patter of Alice's shallow breathing amplifies in the silent classroom. It's like everyone is AFRAID to speak, waiting for the brunette to do something, *say* something. But Alice can't stop smiling, her chapped lips stretched from cheek to cheek, itching to talk, giggle, laugh like a hyena. She's alive, somehow *alive*.

The teacher nods, giving Chloe permission to answer the call.

"No. Mom, that can't be right …"

The brunette's words spill out in a staccato of emotion. Her bottom lip trembles.

Alice shakes her head. *No. Please … no.*

The girl sets her phone on the desk, stares vacantly at Alice, *through* Alice.

"Chloe? Is it your brother?" one girl asks.

A chill settles in Alice's bones.

"We prayed the doctors could save him …" Chloe says, her small voice nearly mute with GRIEF. "But Mom says there's nothing anyone can do."

Her blue eyes cloud with RAGE, ANGER, something eerie and cold. She's no longer staring through Alice, but at her, right at her with absolute HATE.

"They can't save him," she says. "There's no HOPE. It's as though someone has … drained it."

♥

Alice slides down the wall until her ass reaches the gravel, and curls her limp body into a tight ball, pulling her hoodie up over her head to ward off the chill. She wants to cry, knows she *should* cry, but she hasn't come down from the high yet, hasn't stopped

Drunk

floating, hasn't stopped believing in HOPE.
> *There's no HOPE.*

Chloe's words threaten to slap the grin off Alice's face. GUILT has wormed its way in through some tiny pinhole or crack in the armour, winding its way through her blood on a mission to kill Alice, to break
her.
My fault.
She should have stopped long before sucking Chloe's HOPE dry. Should have known to stop.

But now, Alice can't stop smiling: she's grinning like the Mad Hatter at a tea party. She giggles, laughs so hard her stomach tightens and tears fall.
Fall.
Falling for Alice.
She reaches into her backpack and pulls out the stuffed Rabbit and the knife. Flicks open the blade. The steel glints in the waning sunlight. In the mirror-like surface, her face appears distorted, the black circles under her eyes more like elongated ovals. She's crying, blubbering like a fool, still smiling with that wide shit-eating grin.
Crazy, stark raving mad.
Psychotic.
"Oh hey, look, if you're going to kill yourself, do it on the other side of the alley, okay? I have a low tolerance for junkies."

Alice drops the knife. It clatters to the ground hitting the rough-edged asphalt with a *ding-ding-ding*. She looks up through the hood of her sweatshirt and swallows.

The boy is older. Stretched out like Gumby, lean, towering, he's gotta be at least seven feet tall. And muscular, like he's one of those gym jocks on steroids.
Junkie.
His face hides in the twilight; eyes, mouth, nose, all blocked.

Falling for Alice

Alice imagines his features, strong, gruff, and scary, like his voice. She pulls her knees closer to her chest, tucking the Rabbit closer.

"This is private property. Beat it," he says, hitching his thumb backwards, pointing across the alley, to the side that *likes? helps? tolerates?* junkies.

A garbage bag is slung over his shoulder, pushing up against his white chef uniform. Alice's eyes flit to the door wedged open behind him and the spicy scent of Mexican food assaults her senses. "I'm not a—"

"That's what they all say." He reaches down as if to lend his hand and help her stand. "Listen kid, get lost or I call the cops."

Alice doesn't touch him, can't let him touch her. He stares at her with DISGUST, SADNESS, something strange and wondrous. There's no aura around him telling her to stay away, get close, or run as fast as she can.

"Not a kid," she mumbles.

The words hurt her jaw. Her cheeks ache from hours of smiling, her throat raw from laughing, legs weary after skipping through the streets like some happy-go-lucky normal teenager. *Normal.* She licks her lips, thinking about the Chapstick stuffed into her front pocket.

Cherry red.

Alice knows the HOPE she stole from Chloe is fading fast. Too fast. She is spiraling out of control and she cannot, cannot, *cannot* go home like this. Can't let her mother see her like …

This.

"Okay, you're not a kid. Whatever. You can't be here."

The dude crouches, balancing on the balls of his feet. Enormous feet that could crush her like an ant, squash her like a bug. So big, so tall, Alice looks down, away from him, further dipping her face into shadow, as if hiding herself will make him

Drunk

forget she exists.

Eventually everyone does.

He puts his hand on her shoulder instead. His touch is hot, electric, scalding through her thick sweatshirt. Almost chemical. *Zzzzzt.* And for a moment, a glorious, natural moment, the cravings, the thirst, the *need*—

Disappears.

Alice presses herself harder into the wall, wishing she could melt into it, punch through it. Vanish into thin air. *Poof.*

"Don't touch me," she says and tries to stand. Unbalanced, she stumbles and falls forward, falling straight for him, straight *into* him.

He catches her and his hands wrap around her arms, squeeze her tight. The White Rabbit falls to the cement.

Don't touch me. Please.

Touch me.

Somehow, her dark feelings are gone, vanished. She's a blank slate, no pain, no thirst, no ... NEED.

"Steady now," he says, voice gruff. "How much have you had to—?"

"Not drunk," Alice says, CONFUSED. Because she feels drunk. Wasted. Out of her mind mad.

"Are you hurt?" he says.

His words switch from GRUFF to CONCERN, a sudden tenderness that makes Alice wonder if *he's* on drugs. Schizophrenic. Psychotic.

A psychopath.

Alice grabs her knife, the Rabbit, stuffs them both in her backpack and slings it over her shoulder. Turns to run. Run as fast as she can from the alley, this boy, all of *this* ...

Tall, scary, psychopath guy grabs her wrist and she screams. Alice has never heard this noise come from her mouth. It's the voice of a tortured Cheshire cat.

It doesn't scare him off. He's holding her wrist and with every passing second, her FEAR evaporates, melts into nothingness. She can't feel a thing.

Blank slate.

"I'm not going to HURT you," he says, the words echoing in her ears in *sloooow* motion.

Alice yanks her arm free from his grip, flinging her hood backward. The overhead streetlight flickers to life, spotlighting his face, his beautiful, haunting face. High cheekbones, small nose, heart-shaped lips framed with a day's worth of dark stubble, and eyes, cat-like hazel eyes that stare at her, freeze her in place. She's stiller than dead.

Undead.

"Jesus," he says, his voice a whisper of wonder. "You're beautiful."

♥

Alice runs.

She can't go home, not with her hair a matted mess, her eye sockets the colour of soot. Black eyeliner runs from the corner of her eyes to the middle of her cheekbones.

Are my colours too bright
Are my eyes set too wide ...
Teenage Frankenstein.

The further she runs from him, the thirstier she becomes. And as she steps onto the university grounds, it morphs into something dangerous and desperate.

With every step, Alice's ability to hunt, to chase, fades. Her legs tremble, her breath comes in sporadic gasps, the scenery passes in a blur. Green trees, brick buildings, clusters of students gather outside study halls, dorm rooms, converging into one

Drunk

indecipherable hunting ground.

The hair on the back of Alice's neck stands at full alert.

She bumps into a young couple, their heated lovers' quarrel funneling through her blood stream after the slightest touch.

Careful.

The girl flips Alice off.

Alice staggers out of view, out from the direct glow of the overhead lamps. Competing scents layer on her tongue and create a creamy paste of awful.

Ahead, students surround a trio of young hip-hoppers. The air fills with music and explosive energy, a combination of adrenaline-infused HAPPINESS and DRUNKEN CHEER.

Just a little hit. A little something to curb the thirst, to replenish her fading HOPE.

Alice weaves toward the group, elbows her way into the center of the crowd. Almost trips over PRIDE, dodges a shove from a drunk trying to mask DISAPPOINTMENT. She pushes through to the young dancers and stumbles so that she falls into them, knocking the smallest to the ground.

He does nothing, too STUNNED, too wasted to CARE. The music comes to a grinding halt.

She lies on the boy's chest, breathes deeply. HAPPINESS absorbs into her skin through her cheeks, her neck, wherever it can find room. So much, so fast. Too fast, too much. Her body shakes, her temperature spikes. She's burning up, cooling off. Sweaty palms. Dry lips.

Don't stop. Please, don't.

Stop!

Drool gathers in the corner of her mouth, her lips go slack. She can't pull away. She's HAPPY, the HAPPIEST she's been in forever—practically drunk on HAPPINESS. Her father's image, voice, abuse, vanish like a puff of hookah smoke.

And then.

Falling for Alice

The boy jerks his chest to bump her off and grunts.

Alice holds tight.

"Yo bitch, this ain't cool," he says. His drunken CHEER is fading fast.

Alice laughs. She rolls over and collapses onto the damp grass. Voices surround her. *Junkie. Weirdo. Freak.*

Alice buries her head in her hands to block the noise.

A face appears like a mirage through her blurred vision. Somehow familiar. She blinks, opens her eyes, and gasps.

"Jesus Christ. It's you," says the tall, scary psycho with the cat-like hazel eyes.

The world spins like a giant disco ball in a smoky nightclub. A bright light pokes through the shimmery haze of CONFUSION. Alice reaches for it, arms straight, fingers splayed in desperation.

A shadow casts her into darkness.

"I'm calling an ambulance," the boy says.

Alice blinks and the fog fades. He crouches in the grass, looking at her through two glimmering feline eyes. *Why is he following her?*

Alice licks her lips. "No ambulance. Please." Pain throbs at her temples, between her eyes. "I'm sick. Flu. Something contagious, maybe. Go away."

"Right, sick," he says. DISBELIEF creeps along his handsome features, crawls into those eyes and stares at her with DISGUST. "You should go home. It's nine o'clock."

Tick tock.

Tick.

"I can't ... sleep," Alice says.

Drunk

Nine, ten, never sleep again.

She tries to sit up, to push herself into position, but her arms, wrists, her whole body is weak.

"I should just call the cops," he says. He's FRUSTRATED. Alice can tell by the way he talks, the way his body jerks, the clench of his jaw.

Strong jaw. Good bones.

She wonders if he drinks milk.

"No police," she says, lifting herself onto her elbows. A wave of dizziness knocks her back onto the grass.

He offers her his hand.

Alice stares at it, memorizing the pattern of lines across his smooth palm, random creases like clues to his personal life story.

Tell me a bedtime tale.

"I'll help you stand," he says.

"No," she blurts, almost spits out in haste.

Don't touch me. Please.

Touch me.

"I'm fine," she says, avoiding his face. "On my own."

She wants him to leave, to get lost, to go, go ...

Go!

He sits on the grass instead. Long legs crossed and folded like a pretzel. He leans forward and cocks his head. "You're many things," he says, the corner of his mouth twitching. "But fine is not among them. Earlier you're in my alley. Now, at my school." He raises an eyebrow—it's sexy, adorable, charming all at once. "Are you following me?"

Alice shakes her head, hides a small smile. He seems somehow less terrifying under the glowing light of the overhead lamps. Thick clouds slide over the darkening night sky and warn of an incoming storm. She's not dressed for rain, no umbrella, no overcoat to ward off the chill.

Touch me.

"Do you want me to follow you?" she says.

"Not as far as I know," he replies, and even without touching, Alice's heart fills with PROMISE, with something strange and wonderful—TERRIFYING because this combination of feeling is all her own.

She is not touching him. Not stealing his emotions, not draining him.

"You really plowed down that guy," he says. "Are you hurt?"

"I'll live," she says, though the irony of the words does not escape her.

He shuffles closer and points to her forehead. "You're bleeding."

Alice reaches up and touches the skin below her hairline. Hot, sticky liquid coats her finger, drips down to her eyes. She pulls her hand away, shocked at all of the red.

Cherry red.

"Here, let me take a look."

Panic seizes Alice's throat.

Stop. Please.

Touch me.

His fingers caress her skin as he wipes clear the blood, smudging it across her forehead. Her mind goes blank, her thoughts, feelings, the pain.

Blank slate.

"It's just a flesh wound," he says with a laugh, and holds his finger out for show.

Cherry red. Bright and bold and shiny, like a lighthouse beacon. She's lightheaded, dizzy. Ready to faint. She can feel the colour drain from her face. Her pupils darken, transform into black dots. A snowman's coal eyes. She doesn't need a mirror to know that the contrast is SHOCKING. A yin and yang of TERROR.

"You're not going to throw up, are you?" he asks, wiping his

Drunk

fingers on the grass with long strokes. Even his hands are huge.

"It's just blood."

The scent of copper assaults her, like she's sucking on a penny. A trickle of drool escapes from the corner of her mouth. She wipes her bottom lip with her knuckles.

"Jesus," he says. "What are you, a vampire?"

Alice freezes. "Why would you say that?"

Her voice is a whisper. Unfamiliar PAIN squeezes her ribcage, leaving her breathless, speechless, FRIGHTENED.

"Whoa, hey. It was just a joke," he says. His eyes narrow into tight slits. "You're as white as a ghost." He blinks, laughs awkwardly. "Shit, not a ghost, either. Wow. Give me a minute to take my foot out of my mouth. Twice."

Alice smiles.

It's cute the way he fumbles when he talks to her, not gruff, not scary. Almost charming. The tips of Alice's ears tingle.

"Hey. Now that's better," he says. "Smiles look good on you." He punctuates the compliment with a wink.

Overhead, the stars wink back, a reminder of the time, place. She doesn't want to go to sleep, doesn't want to leave.

"So, less like a vampire, then?" she says. Heat blossoms onto her cheeks, face, behind her ears. Where did that voice come from? She sounds so ... CONFIDENT.

Flirty, even.

Alice can't stop the tremble, the vibration of anticipation, nerves, something ... Not. Quite. Normal. He's eyeing her like he wants to gobble her up, go all *Big Bad Wolf.*

As though *he* is the one with the thirst.

Something happens in Alice's belly, a series of tiny somersaults. LUST oozes from her skin, slides from her pores like some creature from the movies. She looks down at the grass, expecting to see a pool of DESIRE at her feet, soaking her high-topped running shoes.

"I'm Lewis," he says, his deep voice bringing her attention back to his wondrous, tortured face.

"Alice," she says. "My Mom mostly calls me A." Alice can't *stop* talking now. Words flow like lava, pour from her lips, red, hot, *over*flowing. "Others call me Allie or Al. I like Alice best. It sounds …"

"Sweet. A little old fashioned." Lewis grins. "Why haven't I seen you before?" The scar beneath his eye stretches as his eyebrow arches.

"You have," she says, smirking. "In the alley."

His expression softens. "Fascinating. Who are you really, Alice?"

"I don't know," she says, cautious and curious. "I'm not the same person I was before."

And it's somehow true.

She runs one finger along her arm, watching the goose bumps pop up from her skin, the small hairs extending like little soldiers. When she gets to her wrist, Alice pinches, hard. Hard enough to make her gasp. She blinks.

Lewis isn't gone.

The thirst hasn't returned.

How much time has passed since her last fix? By now, the first tingles should have kicked in. Is she cured?

Impossible. Any minute now Alice will freak out, have an episode, and Lewis will see—

"I have to go."

"No wait," he says. "Don't leave yet …"

Run.

She can't run.

"I'm okay."

The lie sticks to the roof of her mouth and no matter how much saliva she creates, it won't go back down her throat, won't

Drunk

get off her tongue. Lewis sees it too, the sickly paste of not-quite-the-truth. He won't kiss her now, not before she brushes her teeth, rinses with peppermint mouthwash.

Kiss her?

Alice blurts out a harrumph that sounds more like a dying cat's last breath.

"You're not okay," he says, watching her with an intensity that burns like fire. Hot, so hot. Scalding. "Let me walk you home. You do have a home, right?" His question ends on a hesitant laugh, like he's WORRIED he'll stick his foot, his giant, spider-crushing foot, in his mouth again.

"No, I mean, yes." Alice's response jumbles inside her brain. "I have a home. You don't need to walk me there."

"What if I want to?"

Alice *wants* him to, to hold her hand, to never, ever, ever let go. To make the need, the thirst, go away forever, and always.

He can't.

She is not cured. Not normal.

Alice yanks her arm from Lewis's warm hand. The air is shockingly cold. She turns toward the street, toward home, and begins to sprint, her feet moving faster and faster until the echo of Lewis's voice begins to fade.

Come back.

Wait.

Alice.

The sound is haunting, SAD, so SAD. DESPERATE. Alice wonders if she'll ever get it out of her head, if it will ever—

Stop.

She bends over, hangs her head over her knees to catch her breath. Inhales. Once. Twice. An eerie sensation prickles the back of her neck.

He's coming for you.

Falling for Alice

The thirst has snaked its way back under her skin and now pulses through her veins and arteries, mixing with her blood. Long tendrils of spit creep out of her mouth.
She is a beast.
Paralyzed by thirst.
Alice is dead.
Undead.

Alice dreams of cat-like, hazel eyes, glowing ominously from the pitch-black alley, growing bigger and wider and closer. She breaks out into a sprint, legs pumping, blood pounding, an eerie voice whispering the same thing over and over.
He's coming for you.
He's coming for YOU.
Alice can't move.
She is suspended by rope and no matter how fast her legs spin, her feet don't touch the ground. She's stuck midair. Frozen.
Trapped.
The eyes move closer, turn yellow with each forward step, burning bright enough to cast a soothing aura of light. It forms a halo above the eyes, encircling the blurry form of a head. White teeth, strong jaw.
He's coming for you.
Alice screams, but no sound escapes.
Arms emerge in the darkness and move toward her like a zombie, in slow, methodical steps. She turns her face forward, struggles to break free from the invisible chains holding her in place.
She cocks her head and a face comes into view.
Not a boy, a man.
Daddy?

Drunk

Alice's eyes open. Her heart crushes against her ribs. In the darkness, she reaches for the White Rabbit.

But the Rabbit is gone.

♥

Alice's mother knocks. Her voice is a morning birdsong, too loud, too close. "Sweetheart?"

The voice is tentative, soft.

"Can I come in? I have something for you."

Alice sits upright and pushes the covers, the FEAR away. Her mouth is dry, saliva thick like glue. Her head throbs with the lingering aftereffects of not enough sleep. "I'm awake."

The door eases open. A shadow moves across the floor, causing Alice's throat to constrict, her voice to seize up.

"A boy came by this morning and brought this back for you," her mother says, setting the White Rabbit on the bed. A coolness settles in the air. "He said his name is Lewis. He's very cute."

"He has hazel, cat-like eyes," Alice whispers.

Her mother's hand covers hers in the muted light. "I thought you'd thrown this stuffed toy away. It holds so much…"

PAIN.

Alice sucks in a breath. "I couldn't."

"Because your father gave it to you?"

Alice nods.

"He wasn't a nice man, Alice."

"I know."

"You can't let go of the past, of the hurt, if you're too afraid to move on," her mother says.

Alice clutches the White Rabbit to her chest and the back of her mouth starts to itch.

"Lewis is still downstairs," her mother says, quiet. "He seems … CONCERNED. Should I be?"

Here? Alice's heart begins to thump, slow, steady, until it becomes a rhythmic gallop.

"I'll make breakfast," her mother says. "Should I let Lewis know you'll be down shortly?"

Alice nods. At the thought of Lewis, something stirs deep in her body, her soul.

She can't go *downstairs*. Not yet. Not now.

Not while she is still dead. *Undead Alice.*

Her mother's words echo back at her, forcing her to accept the truth. The realization that her father's LOVE was nothing more than an illusion. And that no matter how much she drinks, how drunk she becomes, nothing can ever fill the emptiness he left behind.

Nothing will ever fully quench this thirst.

Alice stares at the White Rabbit.

And then it hits her.

If she is ever to heal, *to live*, there is something she must do.

The White Rabbit sits in the corner of the closet, pulsating with emotion, with ANGER and HATE.

Alice stares at it, its mocking grin. The red stitching across its heart. Her chest swells, filling up like it's going to explode, implode, go *KABOOM*. Thirst seeps into her blood.

She opens a shoebox and sets the lid carefully on the cool floor. Takes a deep breath. Exhales.

One, two.

He's coming for—

STOP!

She curls her fingernails into the Rabbit's fur, black polish against white stuffing. Her skin prickles, like she's jacked up on adrenaline, overdosing, *drunk*.

Focus.

She stuffs the Rabbit into the shoebox, face up. Its beady eyes

Drunk

watch her, stalk her.

Three, four. Better shut ...

NO! Alice closes the lid, holding it tight, as the tears, the feelings, drip onto the floor. She wraps the box in duct tape, looping it around and around and around until the cardboard is sticky and black.

Lewis.

He's down there.

Alice drags herself from the floor. She is thirsty and weak, vulnerable. SCARED. But Lewis is waiting for her.

She makes her way across the bedroom, every step pushing her further away from the darkness, the White Rabbit, the PAIN. In the hallway, her heart rate increases, and by the time she reaches the landing at the bottom of the stairs, her arms and legs and fingers and toes tingle with—what?

She doesn't know.

Why is Lewis here?

FEAR creeps in through her mouth and winds down her throat, stifling. She stands at the back door, frozen, stiff, undead.

Almost dead.

She sees Lewis through the window. A bouquet of red roses is tucked tight against his white t-shirt. His cheeks and nose have turned pink from the cold. He looks up, and when their eyes meet, he smiles.

Alice gasps. Her throat constricts.

She pushes open the door. "You are here," she says, the words sticking to the roof of her mouth.

He thrusts the roses at her and a single petal sticks to his shirt, a red splotch in the center of his heart. Alice presses her hand against it, waits for the TERROR, the PAIN, the SADNESS to come back, to overwhelm her with emotion. But as his heart thumps beneath her palm, she feels something different.

Something ... alive.

Falling for Alice

Alice. ALIVE. Alive ALICE.

"You fascinate me," Lewis says, and tilts his head so that a lock of hair falls over his eye. *Fascinate.* "I'd like to take you out some time."

Alice swallows. "Like on a date?"

"If you'd like," he says, with an awkward smile. "We could do—anything. Go anywhere."

Alice nods. Her hand is still pressed against his chest, the rose petal glued to her palm. When she pulls back, her heartbeat slows. "I'm thirsty," she says.

"Perfect," he replies, his cat-like hazel eyes twinkling with adventure and mischief. "Drink me."

- THE END -

Alice at Woodstock

by Shari Green

The air-conditioning is broken. I laze on the couch in my family room, sleepy and stupid from the heat, as the afternoon crawls by. My fingers dance on my guitar, messing with random riffs until they settle on one and run it over and over. Max pauses the RPG he's focused on and leans back.

"That's good," he says after a bit.

I don't know what I've been playing.

Max goes back to the game, and I lay the guitar alongside me before snatching a magazine from the end table.

"You're going to swelter in your tux tomorrow," I say, fanning myself with the magazine. "They really should hold graduation in winter."

"Indeed," says Max. "You sure you don't want to be my date?"

I laugh. "Yeah, right—Lewis would love that. Besides, I have to go to my own grad next year, and once is enough for all that fancy crap. But you like that stuff. You'll have a good time."

Max grunts without looking away from the screen.

Until a couple years ago, I mostly hung out with Max's sister, but since she moved in with her boyfriend across town, it's usually just me and Max now. We're practically family, given that our mums are best friends.

"You *did* ask somebody, didn't you?" I say.

"Don't you have a rehearsal to get to?"

I glance at the time. *Finally.* "So why are you still sitting on my floor?"

"I'm leaving as soon as I finish this level."

I abandon Max to his precious game, slip my guitar into its case, and walk the two blocks to Lewis's place. Despite the sweat dampening my t-shirt, I can't keep the smile off my face. When I get there, the garage door is already open. My guitar case slides from my back to my right side, and I lower it to the concrete floor. This is it—the beginning of *our* summer.

Now that school's out, Mad Cat is practicing every day. And then … we're going on tour! Okay, tour might be stretching it a bit, but we've got half a dozen gigs lined up over the next month, and some of them are out of town. The fact we'll barely earn enough to cover gas and keep us in Doritos and iced tea is irrelevant.

Mad Cat is going on tour.

So, why isn't everyone grinning as madly as I am?

"Am I late?"

Dinah busies herself with the drums, her dark purple hair falling forward to form a wall between us. Britt studies the floor at her feet, as if making sure nothing is about to leap up and knock over her mic stand. Lewis stares at me with his gorgeous, nearly-black eyes, and Melissa—what's *Melissa* doing here? And why is there a guitar case at her feet?

Lewis makes some sort of attempt at speech. Not words. He tries again.

"Alice."

Alice at Woodstock

His voice cuts into the fog that's settled in my head. My gaze leaps from Melissa's guitar case to Lew's face.

"I'm sorry," he says.

The last wisp of fog fades away, and realization twists my gut as surely as if I'd taken a swig of poison. Is he really doing this to me?

"You can't cut me from my own band," I say. "I *started* this band."

"It was unanimous," says Britt, and Lewis glares at her.

Dinah glances up. She's crying, tracking jagged black eyeliner-scars down her face. At least this is tough for *one* of them. The others? They don't seem too broken up about thrusting daggers into my heart.

"You make mistakes," says Britt.

"Everyone makes mistakes now and then."

Britt crosses her arms over her chest. "Melissa doesn't."

Heat creeps up my neck into my face, and I've got a death grip on the strap of my guitar case. My throat closes. They're serious about this. One hundred freaking percent serious. My tour, my summer, my dream, my boyfriend—how *could* you, Lewis?—it all vanishes.

I hoist my guitar onto my back. Pushing my way past Britt—and kicking over her stupid mic stand on the way—I bend over my amp, yank the power cord from the outlet, and grab the handle. Then I turn my back on Mad Cat and walk away.

♥

Two months later:

I sprawl on Max's bed, watching him pack. His room is always cluttered, from the overlapping concert posters colouring the walls to the Tonka farm-truck collection scattered over his dresser and bookshelves, but the sorting and packing has amplified the mess. I shift to make room for the pile of t-shirts he plonks on the bed.

"You sure you want to go off and study Agriculture?" I say. "I mean, who studies *Agriculture?*"

Until this summer, I never thought much about Max being a year older than me. But now I have to go back to school and *not* be Alice—lead guitarist of the wildly successful punk touring machine, Mad Cat, that *I* established—and Max gets to go away and live in dorms and study his life-long passion, even if it *is* Agriculture.

Max grins and shrugs his bony shoulders. "Maybe I was a farmer in a previous life."

"You were probably a DJ," I say, indicating his ridiculously huge vinyl collection. "You taking your records?"

"Nah. But I'll write to them every day."

I throw a pillow at him. "You'd better write to *me,* jerk-face."

Max tosses the pillow back.

"I hereby promise to text you everything I learn about environmental science and soil management."

"Oh yay. And you'll do it, won't you?"

"You know I will."

A sigh escapes. "At least you're excited about your future. What have I got to look forward to? Nothing."

"You'll figure it out."

"I'm not good at anything."

"Be a hairdresser." He gestures toward my head. "Nice new colours, by the way."

"Thanks. But no, not interested."

"There's always music."

"Tried that. Failed that."

Max grabs an empty duffle bag and stuffs in a couple hoodies. "I don't get you, Alice. One setback, and you're done?" He

Alice at Woodstock

gestures for me to pass the stack of t-shirts, then he tucks them into the bag. "It's been all summer. Time to get back on the horse."

"The horse?"

"Metaphorically speaking."

My gaze wanders aimlessly around the room, landing on a small toy tractor in the bookcase. I get off the bed and grab the tractor.

"Say you dedicate four years of your life to Agriculture," I say, "so you can live out your dream. Then someone comes along, tells you that you can't plow worth shit and takes away your tractor." I gesture with the toy. "You think you'd be able to get right back on the *metaphorical horse*?"

"That's ridiculous."

"I'm just saying ..."

"You are *not* in a good place," Max says, dropping a handful of books into a box.

"And *you* are not in a very organized place. Who taught you to pack?"

Max scans the disaster. "Clearly, it's time for a break. We need some tunes."

He flips through the albums slowly, thoughtfully, and finally pulls one out. He slips it from the sleeve, sets it on his turntable, and places the needle so carefully you'd think he was setting explosives.

Sound blasts into the room, into my head, into my heart, and I'm right there in the garage again. I slap my hands over my ears.

"No?" Max says, eyebrows shooting up.

I holler over the offending noise. "We did a cover of this."

Max looks blank.

"Mad Cat," I say. "We used to play this all the time."

"Ah," he says. "Sorry."

He puts away the record, and pulls out another. "This?"

"No!"

"Ooh-kay." He slides it back onto the shelf.

"That's one of Lewis's favourite bands."

"You know," Max says, running a hand over the scant blond stubble on his chin, "you can't avoid music forever."

I don't know—I've done a pretty good job so far this summer. My electric guitar hasn't seen daylight since the day my *friends* turned on me, and the acoustic has built up an impressive layer of dust.

"You don't get it," I say. "Music transports me. It takes me back to places and people and memories I don't particularly want to revisit. So, avoidance is good."

Max squats to reach the lowest shelf of vinyl. "What you need," he says, "is something different. Something new. Something that'll take you where you've never been before."

"Such as?"

He holds up a dated-looking album cover. Pink lettering floats above a picture of the band.

"It's time you expanded your musical appreciation beyond punk," he says.

"Seventies? Check out the hairstyles. Yikes."

"Late sixties, actually. And there's a song on it especially for you: *White Rabbit*."

He lifts the needle and moves it to the song he wants, but doesn't lower it. "Lie back, close your eyes, and soak in the magic of Jefferson Airplane."

I hesitate. "What time is it?" My parents hate it when I don't show up for dinner.

"One song," he says.

I pull out my phone. Six o'clock. "I should probably—"

"One song."

I give an exaggerated eye-roll before settling back on his bed.

Alice at Woodstock

"Close your eyes," he says again as he lowers the needle.

♥

Percussion ... guitar ... a rhythm that's unusual, tugging at me as if there's a thread attached to my chest. At first it reminds me of Indian music I've heard, but no ... it's different. Then a woman's voice, a melodic drone, adds another thread, tugs a little harder. The words—something about pills making me larger, other pills making me small, and I don't get it. But then: *go ask Alice.*

So *that's* why Max chose this song for me.

Max slips away. The mess, the boxes, the bed beneath me—it all slips away, and I'm floating on an ocean of sound, the waves lapping, lapping, lapping. The rhythm, the drone, the words, all pulse in my ears, and I can't tell if the music is drifting further away or if it's right inside me.

Acrid smoke tickles my nose. Something scratches at the back of my arms and legs—grass. Damp grass. My eyes flutter open.

Daylight.

And yes, itchy grass instead of Max's quilt.

A guy stands over me, wearing an appallingly bright striped t-shirt and smoking a joint.

"Your head looks like a rainbow," he says. He grins, and it grows to a wide, toothy smile. Then he walks away.

Who *was* that? I must be dreaming. I run a hand through my hair. Geez, it's just a couple streaks ... hardly a rainbow.

I prop myself up on my elbows. I'm near the top of a hill in a huge field—a farm, maybe—and there are people *everywhere*. Thousands upon thousands. The ones near me are spread out a bit, lounging on the grass or on blankets. Farther down the hill, they're packed impossibly close, facing a stage plunked in the middle of this vast field. And the music: that song, *White Rab-*

Falling for Alice

bit, thrums in the air.

This is crazy.

I slowly wind my way through the crowd, inching toward the stage. The band is on to another song, something clashy and post-apocalyptic. I watch the singer—a woman with dark curly hair, wearing white pants and a white tunic with a long fringe. My gaze flicks to the guitarist, then away. The crowd presses in.

Okay, I need to wake up now.

I turn a slow 360. All these people soaking up the music—they all look totally zen. The sound-waves threaten to carry me away again, so I tip my head back, look up, and try to clear my head.

This has to be a dream, but if it's a dream, why can't I wake up? Why can I feel the mucky grass under my feet? (And hey—where are my flip-flops?) Why can I smell the pot and the sweat and the almost-rain in the air? It's real. This field, these people, this freaky-ass music is real. And I've no idea where I am.

So I cry.

I cry a river.

"Hey," says a soft voice.

I swallow hard and swipe at my tears. Through the blur, I see a young couple holding hands—a mousy girl wearing denim shorts and a flowing shirt, and a long-haired guy wearing only jeans. They look my age, or maybe a little older.

"I don't know where I am," I say.

"You're at Woodstock, honey," the girl says. "It's okay. It's a good place. A place of peace, and music."

Woodstock? As in, huge hippie music festival that happened *before I was born?*

The girl lets go of the guy's hand and steps toward me, opening her arms like she's going to hug me. Honestly, I could use a hug. But then, instead of an embrace, the girl takes my shoulders, pulls me close, and kisses me full on the mouth. "Peace," she says as she moves back.

Uh … okay. I stand, stunned, and before I recover, the guy moves in, grasps my shoulders gently, and he, too, kisses me on the mouth. What the hell?

My fingers drift up to my lips. The couple clasp hands again and move off into the crowd, radiating love and peace. And me? Well, at least I'm not crying anymore.

♥

The band finishes their set and leaves the stage, prompting the crowd to rearrange itself. I pick my way across the field. People settle in small groups, sitting on the grass, singing, smoking, sharing food. Couples make out—tangles of arms and legs for me to step around. Laughter rises over the gentle voices of hundreds of thousands of people. How is everyone so *comfortable*? So at ease with themselves and one another? It's like they all know who they are.

The strumming of a guitar lures me, like a folk music Pied Piper. Guitars are dead to me now, but my feet carry me toward the sound anyway, until I'm there, standing over a group of four people. The guy with the guitar looks to be in his mid-twenties, wearing Lennon-style round glasses and sporting at least a couple days' worth of stubble. A girl and another guy—this one heavyset and bearded—lounge on the blanket, singing softly. Across from them, a long-limbed woman sits cross-legged on a guitar case, smoking a hookah pipe. Her hair mingles with the strands upon strands of beads draped around her neck. Hemp cord and more beads encircle her wrist. She lifts the pipe's mouthpiece to her lips, and smoke rises in an elegant dance above her head. The strumming of the guitar continues.

The two who are singing notice me watching them, and they

shift over, opening a place for me next to the guitar case. I lower myself to the blanket. The singing, strumming, smoking continues.

This is totally bizarre.

I don't recognize the songs they're singing, but there's a common *give peace a chance* feeling woven through them. After a while, the music stops, and the girl stretches out, lays her head on the bearded guy's lap, and closes her eyes.

"If only they'd *hear* the message, man," Bearded Guy says.

"We'll keep telling them," the guitarist says. "With protests, sure, but also *with our lives*. Some day they'll see."

A squeaky voice: "See what?"

They both look at me, and I realize the feeble voice was mine. "I mean, what's the message? What are you protesting?"

The guitarist peers into my soul—or it feels like it, at least. "That war isn't the answer. That soldiers armed with weapons and fear isn't the path to peace."

"You mean Iraq?" I say. "Or …"

His brow furrows. "Vietnam."

Vietnam? "Didn't that war start in, like, the fifties or something?"

He nods. "Almost fourteen years now. *Fourteen years.* So tragic, and so unnecessary."

I'm *so* not getting into a political discussion with a guy who thinks we're still in the sixties.

Then again … *Woodstock?*

Max's voice floats into my memory. *Late sixties, actually … soak in the magic of Jefferson Airplane.* This *is* Woodstock. I'm really here—not just the place, but the time.

Whoa.

This just keeps getting weirder.

The guys are talking about plans for an upcoming demonstration, and my attention drifts from their conversation. I turn

Alice at Woodstock

to the hookah-smoking, bead-wearing woman. She rests the pipe beside her on the guitar case and leans slightly forward.

"Who are you?" she asks.

"Alice," I say.

"But who *are* you?"

"Beyond Alice Dodge, you mean?" I shrug. "I don't know. Failed musician. Friendless loser."

There's Dinah, maybe—we were friends long before we were band-mates. But she was part of the rebellion. She didn't have the guts—or possibly the desire—to stand up for me, and I haven't seen her since. So yeah, failed and friendless pretty much sums it up.

"I'm no one, really."

She extends her hands to me, and I notice her bracelets again—so many wrapped and tied on her long arms. She waggles her fingers, urging me toward her. I shift on the blanket and take her hands.

"Tell me more," she says.

Um …

"I was in a band," I say. "But that didn't exactly work out."

Back then—back when Mad Cat was about to break out—I actually *knew* who I was. But now? If I'm not that girl, who in the world am I?

"You know that the past is not really past," she says. "And the present is simply your past's future."

I'm guessing that's not regular tobacco in her pipe.

"Alice," she says, and her eyes lock on mine. "If you want to heal the past, medicate the present."

Seriously? "But that's not healing at all. You can't just *medicate* and hope your problems go away." I restrain myself from adding, *you crazy lunatic*.

"Not *medicate*. Did I say medicate? No. *Appreciate*. To heal the past, you must appreciate the present. Pay attention to it. Be good to it. It *is* your past's future."

That's got to be the most convoluted bit of advice I've ever received from anyone—my mother included. My head may explode.

I want to pull away—shake my gaze from her face, yank my hands from hers—but I'm held there, mesmerized by her crazy-talk. Maybe it's the smoke. Or maybe, something inside me needs what she's offering. Maybe something inside me knows she's not all that crazy.

She goes on. "A musician, you said. So, a creative spirit." She squeezes my hands. "Don't quench the spirit, Alice."

She lets go of my hands, straightens her back, and picks up her pipe.

♥

I wander for what feels like ages, people-watching and constantly pressing down thoughts that the men in white surely must be coming for me, straitjacket in hand. I work my way from one of the huge speaker-towers near the side of the stage, where several people sit balanced in the scaffolding, to way back up the hill, where I first found myself after somehow leaving Max's room. Small tents dot the grass, and the smoke of a couple campfires drifts lazily upward. Something catches my eye near one of the fires: a brightly striped t-shirt. Sure enough, there's an accompanying toothy smile. The guy sees me and raises a hand to wave.

"The girl with rainbow hair," he says when I get closer to him. He jabs a thumb toward his chest. "Charlie," he says.

"Alice."

"Nice seeing you again, Alice." He leans forward, peers at my Ramones t-shirt. "A band?" He straightens up again. "Never heard of them."

He's never heard of the *Ramones*?

Alice at Woodstock

Wait. Late sixties?

"They're … new," I say. "You'll probably hear about them eventually."

He nods, shoots me one of his big smiles, and then flaps an arm in front of his face to push away the campfire smoke that's drifted our way. A guy standing on the other side of the fire raises a green wine bottle to his mouth, takes a swig, and passes the bottle to the woman beside him.

"Looks like it's tea time," Charlie says. "You thirsty?"

My parched and now smoke-irritated throat would *love* a cold drink—preferably a tall glass of iced tea, but I'm guessing that's not actually on the menu.

"No tea here," the woman says. She lifts the wine bottle in a *cheers* motion. "But we've got wine." She takes a drink and hands the bottle to Charlie, who swallows some before passing it to me. I have visions of germs and diseases and other people's spit all mingling on the lip of the bottle, leaping into my mouth, and rushing through my bloodstream, but my hand lifts the bottle anyway, and I'm drinking, and the wine slides over my tongue and down my throat. It's fruity and bitter, not unlike a juice box gone bad, which, sadly, is a taste I know from experience. When the bottle comes around again, I take another sip. Something inside me loosens.

"You're conflicted, aren't you?" says the guy on the other side of the campfire. He's looking at me.

"Why would you say that?" Given my current love-hate relationship with guitars and music, yes—I'm conflicted. Totally. But it's not like I'm carrying a sign.

"Your hair," he says. "Pink stripe, green stripe … like you're making two different statements."

"It's just hair." What is it with these guys?

A drop of rain lands on my arm, and I glance at the darkening sky.

Falling for Alice

"You know," he says, "you probably aren't who you think you are."

I've no idea who I am, nor who I think I am, which is a significant problem, but really? He who judges me by the colour of my hair dye thinks *he* knows me? "I'm pretty sure I'm not who *you* think I am."

"Certainly you're not who I think you are, or who your friends think you are, for that matter. But probably you're not quite who you think you are, either."

"That's true," says the woman beside him. She pokes at the small fire with a stick. "Who *we* think we are, is influenced by who *others* think we are."

"Hence, conflicted," says the guy, and he winks at me.

"That's completely mental," I say.

"*Au contraire.*" He takes a drink of wine, and then passes the bottle again. "I'm Michael, by the way."

"How do I know you're who you say you are?"

He laughs. "Touché."

I spend I-don't-know-how-long with these people, drinking, loosening, contemplating my conflicted state, and, later, watching a nearby woman in a long skirt and halter top work over a tiny camp stove, boiling water in a pot to make … tea. She drops a couple scraggly mushrooms into the water, and I'm thinking that'll be some nasty-tasting tea. She doesn't seem to think so. After a while, she dances to music no one else seems to hear, then eventually finds her way to a blanket and lies down for the rest of her trip.

A man's voice over the loudspeaker startles me. Tiny ant-people mill about on the distant stage, and I realize another band is getting ready to play. Charlie and his grin have vanished.

♥

I should get back. Wherever I am—Woodstock or dreamland

Alice at Woodstock

or the cliffs of insanity—I've been here way too long. But the band starts playing, and I don't want to like it, don't want to get caught up in the music, but the guitarist is so good.

No. Quit listening.

It's too late. It's not just the guitar—the singer's voice has me mesmerized, too. Paralyzed.

Finally, I break out of my trance and move through the totally-peaced-out-on-music crowd, trying to get close enough to the stage to really take in this band. The singer is a guy with long-ish hair and crazy-ass sideburns. He's wearing jeans and a tie-dyed shirt, wailing out a soulful *let's go get stoned*. Okay, not the deepest lyrics, but man, he can sing.

He introduces the next song—with a British accent that was hidden while he sang—and the guitarist is killing it. The singer gets lost in some serious air guitar contortions. I'm watching him for a while before I realize my fingers are twitching. I jam my hands in my pockets.

My traitorous feet pull me closer to the guitar.

Whoa. It's a Les Paul. A *Goldtop*. A freaking Gibson Les Paul Goldtop. They stopped making those way back ... in the past's future? Man, this is confusing. I stare at the guy's hands and that gorgeous guitar until the song ends.

Why am I looking? Why do I care? I'm not a musician anymore. I'm not *that* Alice anymore.

Maybe I never was.

Then again, my fingers seem to remember being that Alice. My fingers want me to leap the fence in front of the stage, grab that guitar—pause to admire and caress it, of course—and then wail on it. Yep, that's what my fingers want, and I'm afraid my heart might want it, too.

Stupid heart. Doesn't it know it'll get broken again? I'm not musician material.

"You play?" The shouted words come from the girl beside

me. "Your hands—they were moving like you were playing guitar. I wondered if you played."

"Not since I got my heart broken."

I can't believe I just admitted that to a stranger. I hate admitting it to *myself*. It's true, of course, and it's not even about Lewis. Losing Lewis didn't break my heart. He didn't cause the deepest wound. Losing the music did.

The song ends, and the British guy stops contorting and stands steady at the mic, talking about the next song.

"I hear you," says the girl. "I'm the *queen* of broken hearts."

I look at the wild roses tucked into her braided hair, scan the face set in an expression of bliss, the eyes that are so far from hurt and angry. Either she's lying, or she bounces back from heartbreak *way* more efficiently than I do.

"You've had your heart broken?" It comes out more incredulous than I intend.

"More times than I remember. It used to be so hard—I'd let some guy steal my song, and I'd be depressed for months."

"Steal your song? And that would be a euphemism for ..."

She looks blank.

"Oh! You mean an actual song. You write songs?"

"No. Not a *song* song." She places a hand on her chest. "My *heart* song, you know? When someone dumped me, I'd feel so bad about myself. All my confidence, my joy, my passion ... gone. But I learned."

The band starts to play—just keyboards.

"Learned what?" I say.

The drums and guitar start, and the girl leans closer and raises her voice over the music. "No matter what happens, don't let anyone steal your song."

She drifts away, but her words linger, winding their way into my mind, seeping into my heart.

My song.

Alice at Woodstock

It's here. It's been right here all along, trying to bubble up, and I *quenched* it. I held it down, but now it keeps flowing out—through my fingers and hands, through my feet, telling me over and over again exactly who I am.

Vocals press in. I blink to clear my head, and I can feel it, can feel joy rising up, pressing against my heart and lungs, and I suck in a huge breath of Woodstock air as I turn my attention back to the band.

I know this song.

What would you do if I sang out of tune ... I might even know this version of it, but maybe not. Maybe someone else sang it. *I get by with a little help from my friends* ... *a little help from my friends* ...

Wait.

What a load of shit.

My so-called *friends* stabbed me in the back. My so-called *friends* yanked my dream right out from under me, and they probably loved doing it. I don't need that kind of help. I don't need friends. And I don't need all this peace-and-music bull.

"Hey!" I holler at the queen of broken hearts. "Hey!"

She looks over and gestures to herself, eyebrows raised in a question.

"Yes, *you*. You're wrong. It's *not* okay—it's never going to be okay."

"I never said—"

"And all you people!" I glare at the people around me, people who have turned oh-so-peacefully to see what the commotion is. "If you think being so freaking *peaceful* is going to fix everything, you're wrong. And who are you, anyway? How are you all here?"

I'm yelling, and crying, and the people—they're moving closer, faces all concerned and caring and shit. "Where am I? Please.

Falling for Alice

I just ... I'm not here. This is insane."

Words and hands, close, so close. *Just a bad trip ... It's okay ...* An arm around my shoulders. Someone's hand stroking my hair, my arm. *We're with you ... You're okay ...* My head spins.

I'm on the ground. My thoughts blur, like a purple haze has filled the air, filled my mind. So many faces. And the music—still, the music. My head reeling, the scene whirling, slowing, fading ...

♥

The music bends, folds in on itself, twists. A familiar melodic drone emerges. Tugs at me. My eyes flutter open.

"So?"

It's Max. Oh glorious day, it's Max. I peer around—band posters and intense clutter all around me, the quilt his mum made beneath me, and Max beside me.

"So what?" I say, hauling myself upright.

"The song. Did it transport you?"

"Oh yeah. You could say that." How long was I gone? Or, dreaming. Or, whatever. I pull my phone out again: six o'clock. "It's only six?"

"It's a short song," Max says. "Told ya there was time for it."

My relief at finding myself in Max's room settles, letting the recent *bad trip* confusion and the old hurt-and-humiliation loser cocktail rush back.

"Why do you stick with me, Max? Why do you bother? I'm weird. And I *am* and always *will be* a talentless, friendless loser."

"Must be your delightful optimism that appeals to me."

I groan. "Sorry. It's just that—"

"Whatever you're going to say, you're wrong. Because music-wise ... I've heard you play. And friend-wise ..."

He shakes his head, leaving that last thought hanging above

the mess in his room. I know he means *him,* and sure, he's a friend, but he's really my mum's friend's son and my neighbour, so maybe he's just a friend by default, and in a different world, he'd never choose me.

As if he can hear my thoughts, Max stares intently at me and says, his voice quiet and serious, "I fell for you a long time ago, Alice Dodge."

Fell for me? As in … ?

Oh.

"I should really get going," I say. "My parents. Dinner. You know." I glance around for my flip-flops. They're probably buried under one of Max's piles of clothes. Forget them.

Max catches my wrist as I head for the door. "I'll come see you before I leave tomorrow," he says.

I nod, and for some stupid reason my eyes water. And then I'm gone.

I dash across the lawn to my house, stopping short when I spot Dinah on my front steps.

"Hey," she says, tucking a long strand of faded-purple hair behind her ear.

"What are you doing here?"

She looks down, hands now hidden in her pockets. "I don't know. Just—" her shoulders hunch then fall "—I'm sorry."

A few seconds tick by, and then Dinah slinks down the steps to the walkway.

She's almost to the street before I react. "You want to go for coffee tomorrow? Catch up a bit?"

She turns back and stares at me, like she's trying to decide if I'm serious. Finally, she smiles and says, "I don't drink coffee."

"Fine. Milkshakes. We'll go for milkshakes." I manage a return smile for my old friend. "You can tell me all about the tour."

After we make plans, I head inside, going straight to my

room. Dad's bound to call me for dinner any minute, but between Dinah and Max and Woodstock, my stomach is crazy-tangled. I need to relax. I close my bedroom door and cross the room to my closet. Reaching up, I shove aside the clothes hanging from the rod, and there it is, propped in the corner: my electric guitar, still hidden away in its case.

Nope. Not ready.

But maybe ...

I shut the closet and take my acoustic guitar from its stand. After using the bottom of my *Ramones* t-shirt to wipe off the worst of the dust, I sit on the floor, back against the bed and guitar on my lap, my bare feet sticking out in front of me.

My *dirty* bare feet.

Yuck. I'll wash off the dried mud and bits of grass later, but now, I tune the strings and strum a few chords. After a bit, my fingers begin to pick out a melody. It's sort of folksy-blues, and it feels good, so I continue. A few words come to me, and I realize the notes and the words have become a song—one of the *peace* songs a guy and a girl were singing on a blanket somewhere in my dreams. I keep playing.

When I go to the kitchen for dinner, I brush past my dad on the way to my spot at the table. He lifts his chin and sniffs the air.

"Were you *smoking pot*?" he asks in a voice that is both accusing and afraid. My mum freezes.

"What?" I say. "No!"

Mum looks from Dad to me, then back to Dad.

"What am I smelling?" he says.

I lift the neckline of my shirt to my face and breathe in. I see a vision of a striped t-shirt and a toothy grin, and yes, there's the lingering scent of weed.

"Not me," I say. "But yeah, I ran into some people who were."

Alice at Woodstock

Suddenly, the truth of it all rushes at me—Woodstock, and making peace, and holding fast to your song, and not quenching the spirit, and finding that you really will get by with a little help from your friends.

My friends—maybe Dinah, who ditched me but came back, hoping for a second chance, and definitely Max, my not-just-by-default friend who's been there all along, reminding me who I am and nudging me to be that person.

I need to be that person.

And I need to see Max.

I excuse myself, ignoring my parents' protests, and race back to Max's place. He's still in his room, still sorting, still packing. He's taking so long to organize his stuff that I wonder if he wants to go at all.

"Hey," I say, out of breath and grinning.

He tucks his desk lamp into a box, and then straightens up. He stands there, a melody of blond stubble, disastrous packing skills, Agricultural aspirations, and that *fell for you* big finish, and he is ... perfect.

"Thought I might've scared you off," he says, and a hint of pink creeps into his face.

I shake my head. "Not a chance."

- THE END -

Playlist for Alice at Woodstock

♥

White Rabbit – Jefferson Airplane

The House at Pooneil Corners – Jefferson Airplane

Let's Go Get Stoned – Joe Cocker

I Shall be Released – Joe Cocker

With a Little Help from my Friends – Joe Cocker

Purple Haze – Jimi Hendrix

She's the One – Ramones

White Rabbit Rx
by Denise Jaden

The second bell rang for classes, and I stood, stunned into place. I couldn't believe I was doing this—not *just* skipping class, but visiting the "office" of the Hatter High drug dealer. This wasn't me. But I had to do it, didn't I?

These three things told me I had to:

1. My weight exploded, out of control—fifteen pounds in less than a month.
2. Nick Wilson dumped me.
3. My only friend made it clear the first two were connected. On Twitter.

@sexydeena: alice chunked out overnight. no wonder he dumped her. #nickissingle

I read the tweet again on my phone, hoping it would bolster my confidence, but my knees were still experiencing an 8.5 on the Richter scale.

I backtracked into the library stacks, wondering what kind

of a drug dealer hangs out in a high school library anyhow. Of course The Pharmacist was no typical drug dealer. Nick purchased his steroids here, but apparently the secretive aspiring med-school student dealt everything from Ritalin to anxiety-relieving tea. I didn't have a clue if he'd be able to help me with a fail-safe diet pill, but I was willing to ask.

At least I thought I was. I grasped a bookcase and wobbled my way toward the window. Maybe I needed the anxiety meds too.

"Hi, I'm Alice," I said to the window, to practice acting calm, normal. "I need your help with this balloon-of-a-stomach, or it's going to lift me up, away into space, and I won't have any oxygen, and then what happens when gravity has no more pull? I'll be an enormous space-bound blimp, floating toward Venus, past Venus, beyond our known solar system!"

I squeezed my eyes shut and put my blinkers on. That's what Deena calls it when I blink hard to reset my mind. She was right about one thing. If I let my jitterbug crazy-talk out in front of someone like The Pharmacist, there was no way he'd take me seriously. I tried again.

"Hi, I'm Alice, and see this stomach of mine? It's not normal. I mean it's huge, it's like I'm housing a baby. Or two babies! Or quintuplets! And all of a sudden I'll have babies erupting out of every orifice and I'll have to quit school and Mom will be a grandmother and have to leave her job to help me … and Deena, she loves babies. She'll visit all the time, every day, probably."

I jammed my blinkers on again, realizing first that I didn't want Deena or my mother to suddenly want me because of my babies, and second that there was no way in the scientifically-sound world that I could be pregnant.

"Hi, I'm Alice," I tried again to the window that was now opaque from my breath.

"Hi, Alice."

White Rabbit Rx

I jumped hard enough to cause the bookshelves around me to stutter. I turned slowly. A guy whisked behind the stacks. I blinked and he was gone, but my recall told me he had glasses. And dark hair. And maybe a goatee.

My gut told me he'd heard more than that last sentence.

Like a creepy stalker, I tiptoed after him, past the first two empty study carrels, and almost barreled into him when he stopped at the third.

He turned and I registered the eight-high pile of textbooks in his study carrel.

"You're pretty funny, Alice." He sat and leaned back, all relaxed. "Need something?"

"Um. Are you ... The Pharmacist?"

His eyebrows launched higher than his stack of textbooks. "Who's asking?"

I looked both ways. "Uh. Me?"

"And you are..." He sounded like such an adult. Not the lanky senior he was.

"Alice."

He blinked. Twice.

"Alice Sanderson?"

"And what can I do for you, Alice Sanderson?"

I looked both ways again, as if I'd find the normal words Deena was always telling me to use scrawled on the sides of the study carrel walls.

"I'm fat," I spat out, then snapped my mouth shut, having the sudden need to erase the reverb echoing through the air between us. "I mean, I've gained lots of weight. Just lately. And I've heard you can make those bodybuilder guys lose weight fast, so I just wondered if–" I trailed off, but he didn't seem willing to fill in the blank. "I wondered if you could help me fix this." I let out my breath. That was almost normal. Wasn't it?

The corners of his mouth quirked up.

"Can you help?" The desperation in my voice scratched like clawing against my prison walls.

"I can help." He pulled a clipboard out from under a mass of textbooks and wrote on a slip of paper. He wrote and wrote and wrote, scribing *War and Peace* or *Moby Dick* or *The Bible*. I wondered if I was dismissed, kept opening my mouth to ask, but then shutting it again, unwilling to give up so easily. I cleared my throat loudly, and he finally looked up. He ripped off the slip of paper and passed it to me.

"Oh!" I took it, filled with a sudden burst of hope. But I deflated just as fast. The writing could've been in English. Maybe. If I had a week to decipher it. Or it could've been Hebrew. Or Klingon. I read aloud the two words at the bottom that I could make out.

"White Rabbit?"

"It's a new drug. Experimental. Not on the market yet, but it will be."

The next words I could make out were "Side Effects," followed by a novel's worth of scribbles. Did he want me to take some experimental drug that could potentially kill me? "This is a … prescription?" I flapped the paper between us to hide my trembling fingers.

He nodded. "Here are the rules: Two hundred dollars, slid inconspicuously into this locker. And don't tell anyone." He pointed at the top of the slip of paper where #1865 was scrawled. "Follow the rules and I'll help you."

I used to float down the halls like a bird, tugged along behind Deena as if on a leash. But now I was an elephant, rattling windows as I took the straightest path to The Pharmacist's locker. How did fat people move nonchalantly? We didn't. We couldn't.

Two students jostled me side to side as they passed, as if I was a bobbly buoy that they had to *bump bump bump* out of their path.

One more thunderous step and I stopped. My thighs took a second to catch up, like putting the brakes on a jackhammer. People looked my way, but lost interest quickly. Not Deena. She was at the far end of the hall and her eyes shot daggers or bullets or missiles at me like *I* was the one who had done something unforgiveable. I reached up to check the back of my head for bullet holes, but then realized I was acting like my crazy self again.

I pushed my hands deep into my pockets, drowning my ten twenties in lint. I wished I could still trust Deena. She and I should be sneaking through the halls, doing our first drug deal together.

When Deena and I met in middle school, shoved together by our alphabetically-similar last names, she assured me that no one would have time for my jitterbug crazy-talk in high school. "Talk like that when we're not at school if you *have* to," she'd said, as if a 12-step program would surely help me shake the habit. "But learn to be normal around everyone else."

I learned to keep my mouth shut and let her do the talking, which seemed like enough normal for her. Until I gained weight.

We were on "the fringe," she told me, which was apparently light years ahead of being in any of those loser cliques. I mostly just felt like we were frogs without a lily pad. Or a pond.

Last week, she gave my body a once-over like I was *below* the loser cliques.

She said, "You've been eating too many tarts, Alice. Maybe you should cut out gluten. My mom stopped eating bread and lost, like, ten pounds."

"I have!" I told her, wrapping my arms around my ever-expanding waist. I thought she was going to help me find a solution, not social-mediatize the problem. The truth was, I hadn't had a tart from the cafeteria in months. I didn't add that, besides gluten, I'd also cut out dairy, eggs, and fruit. I barely ate anymore, and still I was blowing up like a bouncy castle.

Her bullet eyes were still aimed at me. I didn't want to dissolve into a pool of tears for the second time this week, but I had to at least try to get her back on my side. Ever since I'd complained about how much her tweet hurt, she hadn't said a word to me. Now I had nobody.

"Hi, Deena. Hi, Angela," I said as I moved in closer. Angela Watson nudged Deena with her elbow and a silent conversation of eyebrow waggling passed between them.

Finally, Deena faced me. She scanned my body, starting at my feet, and when she got to my face, her lip twitched.

Angela Watson has never liked me. She didn't like Deena either, but that's changed since Deena dumped the dead weight. So to speak.

"Yeah?" was the only word Deena was able to utter when wedged between her popular friend and her crazy ex-friend.

"I'm sorry." I forced out the words, hoping hoping hoping they would bolster a return apology. Her lips tightened like she was waiting for more. She glanced at my hips and scrunched her face at me, as if I'd gained the weight and embarrassed her on purpose. She met my eyes again, raising her eyebrows, but what else could I say? There was nothing to actually apologize for.

My face warmed. Deena had a way of making me feel like she had all the answers, even when I couldn't make any logical sense of them. Hope collapsed within me. She had made up her mind. Our friendship was over.

Without another word, I retreated and took a different hallway. I'd be late for class, but sending two hundred dollars deep

White Rabbit Rx

into the cavern of The Pharmacist's locker slats was obviously my only social hope.

♥

Two days passed and nothing. Spring Break started the following week, and if I didn't get those drugs, who knew how enormous I'd be by the time I came back. Would I even fit through the school doors?

I headed for the library at lunchtime, grabbing my grumbling stomach. There were only three other people within eyeshot, all being swallowed by their open textbooks. A jock emerged from behind a study carrel, stuffing a small paper, likely a prescription for steroids, into his backpack. A shiver ran down my spine as I watched him leave. After my first time meeting The Pharmacist, I paid attention and found out his real name is Solomon—named after the wise one in *The Bible*. A good sign, I supposed, since I'd doubted myself all week for letting my two hundred bucks flutter down the black hole of a stranger's locker.

I slipped off my shoes so my heavy footfalls wouldn't sound so monstrous, tiptoed across the library, and passed the first two carrels.

"Uh, Solomon?"

His eyes honed in on me, then darted in at least three directions.

"Shush! You shouldn't be here again. You want to bring on the heat?"

The heat? "I was just wondering about that prescription," I whispered, forcing my question out fast, for fear of a verbal diarrhea onslaught. "White Rabbit? When will I get it?"

His eyes narrowed. "You sure you still want it?"

"Yes. I'm sure. I told you."

"It's that important, what your friends think? You really want to do this?"

Falling for Alice

"Yes!" Panic seeped into my voice. I was *this close* to screaming at him, at the library, at the whole world, that I didn't have any friends anymore. I quelled my energy and repeated it quieter. "I do."

"What's your favourite colour?"

"Blue, I guess."

"Favourite movie?"

My …? What on earth did this have to do with a diet pill? "*Alice in Wonderland?*"

"Worst nightmare?"

"This! Right now. My life!" I stopped trying to hide my exasperation. Was he as crazy as me?

He nodded slowly. "Okay. You'll know when I know."

I glanced over my shoulder, but couldn't see anyone from here. "But, I mean, it's almost Spring Break, and it doesn't make sense. You don't have my phone number, and I don't even know you or how you plan to get it to me."

"It doesn't make sense?" Solomon said, drawing out the words. "Nothing makes sense, unless you look at it the right way." He passed me a small mirror from one of his binders.

I looked into it, then squinted back at him. He watched me carefully. Did he want me to realize just how large I'd become?

"I needed to confirm you were sure." He snatched the mirror back. "I have my ways to deliver. Relax, we're very close. Now run along before word gets out, and everyone wants their own little white rabbit." His mouth and eyebrows tugged high on his face, and I couldn't tell by his wide eyes if he was joking or serious. "Besides, you don't want to be late, right?"

There were still twenty minutes left of lunch, but I backed away with a slow nod.

♥

I spent the afternoon wondering if I had given my last two hundred dollars to someone no more mentally competent than I was. I stared diagonally across my English class at Nick, hoping for a distraction.

I wasn't the first unpopular girl he'd gone out with. It seemed to be his "thing." Before Angela Watson went out with him last year, no one at this school knew who she was. Nick and Angela dated for a few weeks, didn't seem serious, and it gave her a step up. He'd done that with at least three girls on "the fringe," so Deena assumed it would work the same way with me. Nick and I had walked the halls holding hands a few times. We had planned to go on a date when he found some free time between practices.

But week after week passed, and before I realized what was happening, I'd gained weight. A lot of weight. And instead of taking me out, he'd dumped me by text.

It's not going to work out with us, Alice. Sorry.

I was sad, but not nearly as devastated as Deena. That was when she started going on about all the tarts I was eating.

♥

Hatter High cleared out faster than a vampire clan at sunrise when the final bell before Spring Break sounded. I, on the other hand, strolled through the halls, scuffing my feet and twirling my hair. It wasn't like I had anywhere to be or anyone to walk with.

The hallway was practically empty by the time I swung open my locker. I immediately stepped back. A puff of white, like a gallon of cotton batten, poofed out from the bottom. Some kind of animal? I hesitated, then poked the mass with my pen, ready to jump away if it moved. It collapsed into my mass of binders, ears flopping forward, and I realized it *was* an animal. A stuffed one.

Picking it up, I studied the stuffed rabbit. The stuffed *white* rabbit.

Falling for Alice

I glanced down the empty hall. Was this some kind of a joke? Did I just pay two hundred bucks for a glorified Beanie Baby? The thing was as soft as flower petals, but for two hundred dollars, it had better come with a spa treatment or a lifetime supply of chocolate.

I should have known by the nonsense Solomon spouted the last time I'd talked to him. Maybe he wasn't truly The Pharmacist.

Holding the rabbit by one ear, I walked it across the hall to the nearest garbage can. My anger at Solomon, and at myself, pulsed through my arms and into my fingertips, and I was about to release them, let the rage go, when the swinging rabbit turned slightly to reveal its belly.

A zipper.

I caught the rabbit before it landed in the heap of trash. I gave the guts of the thing a squeeze, and sure enough, there was something hard and round inside.

I unzipped the belly. A vial!

I checked the hallway for people again, and rushed back to my locker. There was no dosage listed, no official looking prescription sticker, only two simple words scrawled on the glass vial in Sharpie.

Drink me.

I ducked my head into my locker. *There's no one around*, I reminded myself, then pulled out the stopper and sniffed it. I grimaced at the smell, a mixture of mushrooms and cake. I plugged my nose and put it to my lips before I had a chance to gag or second guess.

If there was a taste, I didn't register it. Quite suddenly, I lost all sense of balance, falling into my locker, forward and down down down.

I blinked into the darkness—once, twice, and the third time extra hard.

White Rabbit Rx

When I opened my eyes, it was bright, motion all around. It took me a second to realize I was strutting through the front doors of the school. I blinked hard once more, but everything continued to move. *Everyone* was in motion. The hallway was now filled with students.

And people looked at me. Lots of people.

What the ...?

Involuntarily, I lifted a hand to wave back to three popular girls who said, "Hi, Alice," as if they knew me.

I wrapped my arms around my waist, to cover myself like I always did, but my arms slid around to my back.

And my jeans. They weren't my jeans. There was no stomach pushing past them.

I knew there was something very different—very skinny— about me. Not only that, but I was wearing the cutest little capris—the kind I'd never even glance at in the mall. When did I change clothes? But before I could answer all of my questions, my mouth stretched into a wide grin.

White Rabbit was truly a miracle drug.

I walked forward with my head held high, locking eyes with Deena at the far end of the hall. I tried to ignore the fact that there shouldn't have been any people here. Deena and the rest of the students should've been at home for Spring Break. But I didn't dare question it.

But then, just as suddenly, I didn't feel so good. I stopped at a nearby locker to regain balance.

On Solomon's illegible prescription slip, he'd listed all the possible side effects for White Rabbit. I'd spent the last week deciphering and memorizing every word of it. Headaches was at the top of the list.

I shut my eyes now, and the first thing I tuned into among the chatter was Deena's voice. I peeked and she was definitely at the far end of the hallway. But I could still hear her talking as if she was right beside me.

Plus the smells. Sweat and paint and perfume overwhelmed me.

I pulled the prescription out of my pocket and skimmed past headaches, dizziness, and nausea. My finger stopped on "heightened senses."

I stared down the hall to where Deena was speaking to Angela, but the chatter all around me had become so loud my head felt like it was going to split in half. I closed my eyes and tried again. This time, it wasn't Deena's voice I heard first. It was Angela's.

"She's lost so much weight. Too much weight, I think. Don't you think she's too skinny? She must be bulimic."

"Totally," Deena said. When I opened my eyes, they were coming closer.

"Hi, Alice," they said in unison, smiles pasted on their faces, like they hadn't just been criticizing me.

"Um. Hi?"

"See you at lunch?" Deena said, as they passed.

I watched them walk on, stunned.

"You okay, Alice?" Solomon stepped into my vision.

I looked both ways, remembering he shouldn't be seen with me. "Yeah. I think so." I blinked hard, mostly to clear my head, but this time my tuning to their voices was immediate.

Deena: *Oh my god, look who she's talking to! Do you think she's into drugs or something?*

I opened my eyes and Solomon was reaching out to touch my shoulder. I took a giant step away, leaving his hand stuck in midair.

"I'm fine." I took another wobbly step back, wondering how Deena even knew Solomon was The Pharmacist, and why she'd never told me about him. Didn't matter. I wasn't about to get him caught for helping me. I took another step away, but Solomon shadowed me.

"It worked." He scanned my body up and down, but his gaze didn't feel as scrutinizing as when Deena did it. "Did you get used to it over Spring Break?"

Spring Break? Did I completely miss Spring Break? I shook my head slowly. "It's like I'm super-charged. The voices and smells ..."

He tilted his head, like he was trying to see something behind my eyes, and flashed that quirky smile of his. "Come to the library at lunch?"

"I—I can't," I said, looking toward where Deena and Angela were still studying us. Maybe everyone liked me because I was skinny now. Maybe even Solomon was willing to be around my new skinny bod. But I wouldn't get him caught.

He moved in close enough to catch my arm. "Aquamarine, The Matrix, and this time when I was taking the SAT and earwigs were crawling all over my test so I couldn't see the questions."

My eyes widened. *Why was he saying all of this nonsense?*

As though I'd posed the question aloud, he answered me. "This is what friends do, right? They tell each other things about themselves."

Things about themselves. Like ... their favourite colour. Their favourite movie. Their worst nightmare.

"I—I don't know what friends do," I blathered. Then I scurried away before anyone else could see us together.

I spent my first class, biology, trying to figure out this new superpower of mine. I had to shut my eyes to focus, and couldn't always control what my enhanced senses picked up. For example, I really had not wanted the enhanced version of Cameron

Falling for Alice

Renaldo's fart.

Between classes, I moved through the sardine-packed hallways with a brand new ease, getting to my classes with time to spare. I didn't even have to spend the usual thirty seconds catching my breath at the doorways to my classes.

I kept my ears open and learned about upcoming parties I normally wouldn't have heard about, a cheerleader who was about to be dumped from the team, and I confirmed that Angela and Deena both felt jealous of me. *Me!*

The headaches, dizziness, and nausea only came on when I tried to hear stuff I shouldn't be able to hear, so as the day went on, I tried focusing in smaller chunks. But teachers were calling on me more and more often. It was as if they hadn't been able to see me when I was hidden behind my frumpy self. I wondered if it would be the same with my mom. If she would finally notice me again. My feet and legs twitched below me, fresh and full of energy. I considered skipping the school bus and jogging home right after school to find out.

When I could tune in to the students' voices around me, they were getting louder, taking over each other, and it was becoming hard to pick them apart.

Curiouser and curiouser.

Nick took his seat diagonally across from me in English class, among the other jocks. He glanced my way. As I blinked, his cologne made me cough.

"Hi," I mouthed, waving a slow hand at him. I let him look at the New and Improved Alice, grinning again from ear to ear about all the ways my life had transformed.

An ambiguous Cheshire grin spread across his face.

When he turned to his friend, I tilted my head and shut my eyes. A mesh of guys' voices followed.

White Rabbit Rx

Guy #1: *You seen Alice, man?*

Guy #2: *Yeah, she's lost a lot of weight. She looks hot.*

Nick: *She does, but whatever. I'm keeping my eyes off of her and all girls. You heard what coach said about me dating.*

Coach? When the guys talked again, they were quieter and I had to concentrate hard to hear them over the teacher's voice.

Guy #1: *Coach don't have to know. 'Sides, nobody said anything about dating her.*

Guy#2: *I don't know. Now that I'm looking, most've her boobs are gone. Her pants are hanging off her.*

I peered down, and maybe it was true. The capris looked looser than they did an hour ago. Too loose.

Guy #1: *I'd still do her.*

Nick: *You guys are killing me..*

"Am I putting you to sleep, Alice?"

I jumped in my chair at the sound of Mr. Montgomery's loud voice. Slowly, I opened my eyes, and blinked away the brightness.

I squinted, trying to ward off the headache. "Oh no, Mr. Montgomery."

"See me after class, please, Alice."

In gym class, I had unending energy, carrying so much less weight around. But then I started to hear voices clear across the gymnasium, and even from the hallways, and it became impossible to tell who was actually talking to me, and who was having a private conversation in another part of the school. Then I got knocked clear over by a basketball that was gently tossed my way. I suddenly had no strength, and when I got sent to the nurse's office for my fall, three people I'd never spoken to before offered to walk with me.

The school nurse gave me a stern talking-to about eating disorders and released me right as the lunch bell sounded.

Falling for Alice

I was trying to decide between eating with Deena and Angela, even though they'd been talking behind my back, or hiding out under a stairwell, but when I left the school office, at least fifty sets of eyes darted to me.

"Hey, let's go for lunch, Alice," said a girl I didn't even know.

Another girl pulled at my arm, and I swore it was going to pop right out of my shoulder. "She's sitting with us today."

From down the hall, Deena tipped her head toward her and Angela. They both flashed genuine-looking smiles.

While I was focused on Deena, Nick sidled up beside me. "Hey, Al." He had never called me Al before. "The guys are wondering if you want to sit at our table today."

Not him, but *The Guys*. I had barely opened my mouth to decline when two of his friends near the cafeteria doors, who I shouldn't have been able to hear, started discussing which one of them would sit beside me. Which one of them wanted to "do" me now that I was skinny. I took a step away from Nick, away from everyone, and raced for the exit.

We're not allowed off school grounds during lunch, so I stood outside in the rain, around the corner from the front entrance blinking fast, wondering what on earth just happened. People were drawn to me, but not in a normal friendly way. Those people weren't my friends. In fact, none of them even seemed to care when they were hurting me.

I wrapped my arms around myself to fight the cold, but it was no use. I couldn't seem to keep this skinny body warm. It didn't help that my clothes were getting looser and looser as the day went on, letting in plenty of airflow beneath them.

I waited until the outside monitor turned his back and skirted behind the school, hoping the door near the library was open.

♥

White Rabbit Rx

"You need to fix it."

Solomon looked up at me from his library carrel and blinked a few times. He smiled. "Alice."

"Look at me, it won't stop. I'm getting skinnier and skinnier, and the voices are caving in my head. Soon I'll be breaking bones just from walking." My mouth went dry as the truth of my words hit me. For once in my life, I wasn't overdramatizing anything.

Solomon squinted. I hadn't even noticed if there was anyone else in the library. At the moment, I didn't care, because if he was like everyone else, only liking me because I was skinny now, he probably wouldn't care about hurting me either.

"But this is what you wanted," he started. "I tried to tell you not to—"

"I know you tried to tell me and I didn't listen. And I know it seems crazy to not want to be like this, but I want to go back to how I was!"

"You want to be ..."

"Fat. Yes! Even if I don't have any friends, at least I'll know I'm not going to fall apart in a pile of brittle bones in the middle of the floor. At least I'll know people are genuine. I'm really okay to be fat and crazy, even if no one likes me that way." I didn't think Solomon would understand, but he nodded as if maybe he did. Or at the very least, he knew *I* believed what I was saying.

Solomon paused, but then reached behind his stack of textbooks for a Styrofoam container. In Sharpie along the top, it read, *Eat me*. "If you take them too close together, I can't guarantee ... I don't know what will happen."

Even though it looked like one of those hamburger cartons from the cafeteria, a carton he was trying to hold back from me so he'd have it for his own lunch, I snatched it out of his hands.

Falling for Alice

"Don't worry, I'll leave you alone now." I told him. "I know how this 'friendship' thing works."

♥

I stood at my locker for five minutes before I could wrap my head around eating cake. I had programmed my brain to reject anything with any caloric value. Plus, look what happened the last time I ingested something Solomon had given me. I looked at the mound of fluffy yellow cake, thick with sugary white icing, and told myself I needed the added weight. Desperately.

I had only taken a single bite of the fluffiness when everything in my vision blurred in slow motion. Students and hall monitors moved like caterpillars down the hallway. I dropped the Styrofoam to balance myself against my locker. Dizziness overwhelmed me and I fell forward.

I tumbled down and around.
Darkness.
"Alice? Alice?"
I heard my name, but couldn't see a thing.
"Solomon?" I squeaked.
A pull to my hand, and I was yanked into the bright yellowy light reflecting off my locker. Had I fallen inside?

"Alice? You're okay? I came after you to tell you not to eat the whole thing."

I glanced down to where the nearly full slice of cake had dropped to the dirty linoleum floor. From there I noticed my ankles, thick under socks and tight jeans, my thighs, filling in all the wrinkles.

"I'm me again." I whispered. My bones felt strong. My clothes were comfortably snug.

"Yes." Solomon smiled. "You seem happy." He tilted his head. "Not like you're a space-bound balloon or housing quintuplets?"

White Rabbit Rx

I felt my face flush. He remembered all that jitterbug crazy-talk of mine from when I'd first come to see him?

"You shouldn't … You shouldn't be seen with me." I murmured the words, cowardly, like the Alice who used to hang out with Deena. Because the truth was, it would be hard not to have at least one friend. But I was still glad to be normal. Or at least my kind of normal.

"Why not? We're not doing anything wrong here in the hallway." As he spoke, he picked up the cake, and threw it in the nearest garbage. He obviously meant we were no longer dealing drugs.

"But no one likes me." I motioned around to the slow trail of students, headed off to fourth period, none giving me a second glance. "They won't like you either."

He shrugged. "People will always like me. I have something they want."

It was probably true. He'd always be popular, but it surprised me how much he sounded like he didn't care. I nodded, but backed up a step.

"People would probably like you too, if you showed them how interesting you are." He took a step toward me. Deena never liked the interesting side of me. But maybe … maybe Solomon really was okay with my ostracized self, my jitterbug crazy talk. "Sometimes people like us for the wrong reasons," he added.

True again. Even Angela Watson seemed to like me when I was skinny.

"Maybe I'll see you tomorrow, hey, Alice." It didn't seem like a question. "We could talk about colours or movies."

"Or earwigs," I said, remembering his nightmare about taking the SAT. I wanted to hear more about that.

He grinned. Nodded. "Yes, definitely the earwigs."

Falling for Alice

Maybe I was only a science experiment to him. Or maybe he actually found something about my craziness endearing. I glanced down at my body—bigger, yes, but healthier-looking. My skin was a nice beige, not the grey I'd been when I was skinny.

Maybe I shouldn't want to be friends with the school drug dealer. Or maybe, for the first time, I'd finally found the best kind of friend.

The Pharmacist. My real live White Rabbit.

- THE END -

Wormhole to Wonderland

by Kitty Keswick

Stardate: 2114

Small meteorites pinged off the hull of the Starship Jabberwocky, class *A* terraformer, skipping through the thick blanket of ice and debris from a long forgotten star. Pinballing off each other, they disappeared as flashes of fiery comets, drawn in by the twin moons' gravitational pull. Two days ago, our spacecraft had reached the assembly point, Kepler-22b, a habitable planet six hundred light years from Earth in the Cygnus Constellation.

My breath fogged the glass. I traced shapes on the cold surface using my fingertip, connecting the twinkling dots to form an H. Without thought, I drew a heart around it. Paused, and cocked my head, studying the art I had created. I winced and rubbed the space between my eyes.

Over the last few days, the twinge at the back of my head had graduated from a dull ache to stabbing annoyance, coupled

Falling for Alice

with the tinny taste that still coated my tongue. Worse than the pain was the sense of disconnection, as if puzzle pieces in my head were plucked away and removed. Hypertravel was hard on fragile human bodies.

"Alice, you're going to be late." The metallic voice of my A.I. (Artificial Intelligence) guide, Dinah, was sometimes akin to nails on a chalkboard—always riding me about something. Yet, I was comforted knowing she (I assumed the robot was female) was there for me, no matter what. In a way, Dinah was my mother, sister, and friend, all rolled up into a shiny white almond shape of annoyance.

Dinah flew to the window and wiped my doodle clean. Always worried the Originators were watching—not to mention Dinah was a bit of a neat freak.

"I'm so tired," I said. "Mind melds make my head spin. I can't possibly have another novel streamed into my thoughts tonight."

Dinah hummed in a high pitch as if she'd blown a circuit. I'm sure Dinah's circuit's were smoldering, fed-up with my whining, sick of my defiant ways. A.I.'s weren't used to disobedience.

I was the fourth of twelve females and twelve males in the Alpha class. Our embryos were unfrozen fifteen years ago as our Starship dropped out of warp speed nearing its destination. Twenty-four souls occupied this ship, each given a designation, a purpose, and the appropriate training to start a new world along with another twenty-three terraforming ships.

Heady crap.

My designation was literature. In other words, my DNA was harvested and blended with that of the great authors of my long gone world. All the authors' DNA samples were used in my creation, I was the last of my kind, the only one with true creativity and the ability to think. Which got me into a lot of trouble,

Wormhole to Wonderland

sometimes—okay, most of the time. Dinah said I was prone to daydreaming and often needed my programming checked. Translation: she'd love any excuse to shut me up— or redirect my creative energies to more productive means. I could parrot that line back to her word for word and match her tone. Each day, twenty-five to thirty novels were uploaded via the data port at the back of my neck. I studied voice, pacing, metaphors, and similes, dissecting the written word until the letters blurred and jumbled my thoughts and pulverized my brain. Soon I'd be responsible for creating stories of my own, giving our new world an "escape." I couldn't wait to explore my ideas, share my stories with others, be a real writer. The Originators were only obeying our ancestor's wishes by having my *kind* on board. One of the major backers of the terraformer project was a *New York Times* bestselling author. My peers didn't think my talents were as important as spacecraft propulsion, or gravitational acceleration. I'd rather be creative than recite *Newton's third law of motion*, any day.

I knew all about that and more. After having an entire library of novels and textbooks uploaded into my brain, I craved adventure of my own. Mystery. Romance. Heck, I'd even trade a vanilla flavored MRE for a space odyssey … anything that got me off this spaceship.

I ran my fingertips under my hair along the scarred skin at the back of my neck. The thumbnail-sized data port itched like the Cheshire cat had given me its psychedelic fleas.

Our ancestors commanded twenty-six starships in the hopes that by separating us we'd have a better chance of survival. Space was a dangerous place. We'd lost all the ships but mine. I was humankind's only hope for a future life on an unknown planet. Humans had destroyed Earth, polluted its rivers, clogged its skies, and killed its wilderness.

Big problems! And yet, I had homework.

Falling for Alice

"Alice, I insist you follow protocol," Dinah said. A blue light washed over my body. "My sensors show increased activity in your occipital lobe, you could experience sensory overload and I'm getting a strange reading in your temporal lobe, it appears some of the memory pathways are blocked. I should escort you to sick bay."

"I'm fine, Dinah." Truth was I felt a bit odd. I couldn't piece it all together. But, the last place I wanted to be was sick bay. That place ...

"Alice. You're not functioning at full—"

Ignoring her, I stared out the porthole, turning to the side, marvelling at how the craters of one of the moons seemed to form the shape of a rabbit.

Dinah flew in front of me, blocking my view, and then to my side, hovering at eyelevel. A series of blinking blue lights created a crescent shape reminiscent of a smile. Just below the crescent was a small indentation. I flicked my finger out and quickly depressed it. The blue lights flashed and then winked out. I caught her before she hit the floor, and set her safely onto the spaceship floor. She'd reboot herself in a few moments and be as annoying as ever. At least I had a moment to myself to think, to daydream, to just be me.

No protocol.

No rules.

No masking my abilities.

A click and a pop sounded off to my left. Turning toward the display case that housed relics from our past, the door swayed slightly with the movement of the ship.

It's always locked.

I moved to investigate. Dinah's voice echoed in my memory: *Curiosity is a blessing and a curse—it killed the cat.* She had an opinion about everything.

I stood before the display case. When I was little, my head

Wormhole to Wonderland

barely reached the bottom of the wall-mounted cabinet. Inside were things that belonged to my ancestors—daily items to them, now precious to me. The last of their kind. Every artefact was arranged plainly, a teapot with a small chip on the spout, two matching cups with mismatched saucers, a top hat with worn ribbons around its base, two silver button hooks that needed a good polishing, a brass spyglass with worn leather straps—I itched to use that personally ... and—

Crap! Where was it?

The stuffed white rabbit was gone.

Through my peripheral, I caught a flash of fur. I spun around just as a cottontail turned the corner and disappeared down the grey corridor. "How odd," I said. Stuffed rabbits didn't *move*. It reminded me of the novel by Lewis Carroll, *Alice in Wonderland* about a girl that shared my name— I'd uploaded it just last month. And joked with someone about ...it all seemed so foggy.

Blood pumped in time with the pounding pain in my head. Still, I felt drawn to follow.

The white rabbit hopped along the grated floor keeping several paces ahead of me. Its fur wasn't that same matted faux-fur, grey with age. Now its fur matched the polished sheen of the white walls of the corridor, glossy and lustrous. I wondered what the fur would feel like under my fingertips. Soft. Subtle. Delicate. So life-like, I rubbed my eyes in disbelief. No matter how fast I scurried after it, it leapt ahead. Determined to catch the creature I picked up speed. A door slid open leading to the restricted airlocks. I didn't have security clearance but wasn't about to argue the free pass. Curiosity had always plagued me—Dinah told me I came by it naturally because of the creativity built into my DNA. Dinah had rattled off statistics measuring my rate of disobedience to the probability of the Originators finding out that I'm different. Her numbers are not in my favour. I'm care-

Falling for Alice

ful, enough. Nevertheless, if I didn't know better I'd say my A.I. is a worrywart.

Impossible since she's all circuits and lights, right?

I'd been able to figure out most of the Starship's secrets and finally could add another. I hurried down the passageway leading to the ship's underbelly and caught another glimpse of the illusive furball as it hopped up to a sliding glass door. The door slid closed with a loud whoosh. The white rabbit continued down the corridor, disappearing through a small opening. I ran after it.

Strange lights glowed from within the opening. I knelt and peered inside, only to be sucked ...

Down
    down
        down I fell—
            into nothingness.

Something sharp shot against my skull as I continued tumbling, ass over ankles, through an electric blue force field like webbing. Pain radiated across my forehead. I rubbed the spot as it numbed.

Ahead, the stuffed rabbit created a fluffy jet trail of grey-blue. Reaching for it, I somersaulted and hit a dip and curve as the wormhole continued. Every now and then, I caught a glimpse of the brilliant blue illumination at the end of the tunnel. Knowing there was an end, I relaxed and reached both arms out to touch the sides. My fingertips caused the webbing to spark.

I giggled to myself. This was the most extraordinary event I'd ever seen.

The floral teapot wheeled past me, lid nowhere in sight. I reached out to grab it, only to have it slip through my fingers, creating another jet trail as it whizzed ahead. Something tickled my arm, soft and plush. A top hat whirled like a leaf on the

Wormhole to Wonderland

wind. It too zipped ahead.

I wondered where it would take me. Part of me didn't care. I felt free, finally on an adventure of my own. Thousands of possibilities flooded my mind—stories I itched to write. Not simply recite the uploaded ones. I longed to look at life through the wrong end of a telescope, to speak nonsense, to laugh when it wasn't called for … live every day as a fantastical journey. Each step unscripted.

Stars and celestial bodies flourished as brilliant flickering lights in a Kaleidoscope of rich yellow, vibrant oranges, and deep fiery reds. I gasped—floored by the beauty—and did my best to commit the colours to memory.

Hurry Alice, it's your only hope. I thought I heard Dinah's voice crack through my communication pin.

No time to think. I landed with a thud. I rubbed my elbow. I'd smacked my funny bone when I landed and the pain snaked up my arm in a burning path.

The chamber was cylindrical by design, created out of metal hexagons and along the base every few feet, small black holes had been cut into the metal. There didn't appear to be a way out, and travelling upwards from where I came wasn't a feasible option. Trapped! But where? Another spaceship?

Claws scraping against metal sounded from my left. A few feet away from me, the rabbit sat and twitched his nose. I reached for it, relieved it was still in sight, only to witness the end of its tail disappear as it hopped through a black hole in the cylindrical wall. The animal had grown—almost doubled before my eyes—and as I dove for it, the hole shrunk to the size of an apple.

I slammed my fist against the tiny metal door frustrated that the rabbit had once more eluded me. If it could get in maybe, I could, too. My fingers dug into the metal around the opening

Falling for Alice

and I pulled, and pulled and pulled. Nothing happened. Well, except my frustration level rose tenfold.

"You won't get through there without a key," an echoy male voice said.

I rolled over and sat up. "Who said that?"

"You need a key."

"I'm not going to speak to you until you stop hiding," I said, swallowing, and hoped that my voice didn't sound as tiny and scared as I was starting to feel.

"You seem to be speaking fine. You need the key anyway."

"I don't have one," I said. I cracked my neck and shook out my arms. The impact made me feel as if hundreds of tiny meteorites pulverized my body. I glanced around the room.

Neat rows of equally spaced iron hexagons melded the metal walls together, and they didn't offer any clues for an escape route. Where was I? Was I still on my spaceship? It didn't feel like it. Would I be stuck in this room forever?

"You haven't looked very hard, have you?" the voice continued.

"There isn't anything in the room but me."

"Claptrap, complete Balderdash, there's a lovely table in the centre of the room."

I turned, and true to the voice's word, there was a table. I walked to it and ran my hand along the dents and scars in the walnut wood. It felt real. I'd never felt wood before but knew what it looked like from pictures. My world was plastic, metal, and glass. Manufactured. Cold and sterile.

"I see the table. It's empty."

"Is it? My, my, girl, you truly need to look closer at things." The voice echoed off the metal walls from every direction, travelling through to the soles of my feet. I stepped back and bumped the table. Something slid across it.

An iron key with a long shank, decorated with a climbing rose.

Wormhole to Wonderland

"That wasn't there before," I said.

"It's always existed."

I picked up the key and ran my finger along the cold metal. Solid—not a figment of my imagination, at all.

"I must be mad," I whispered.

"Perhaps. Madness seizes the best of us. You wouldn't know it if you were truly mad, would you? That is madness' secret—it comes like a thief in the night and steals your mind."

I glanced at the key. It had to fit a lock. Kneeling, I searched all the small round holes. A finger length into one of the holes, I felt a solid mass and ran my fingertip over a keyhole. The rabbit was going somewhere. It seemed purpose drove it. I *needed* to know where. I felt the craving so thick in my bones, as if it was encoded into my DNA. The pull to follow was enormous. I had an inkling that the rabbit might be my key, my way out of this place. I wanted my own Wonderland. Sliding the key into the lock, I turned it until it clicked. The door opened inward—but it was only about the size of my fist. Peering through, I watched the rabbit dart down an empty corridor.

With each failed attempt, the walls seemed smaller. The thought of spending all eternity in this tiny room, sent the sensation of ants crawling along my flesh. I sucked in the panic. "The key to a small door is completely useless," I said. "I'm tired of these games. Tell me how to get out of here!"

"Through the door. Of course."

"I. Cannot. Fit."

"Not at that size. You must be smaller."

I threw up my hands and paced. "Obviously."

Pain radiated at the back of my neck. Legs wobbling, I collapsed.

Dinah's voice whispered through my communication pin: *Alice, Alice stay with me.*

A memory flooded back. One *they* thought they'd erased.

Falling for Alice

Hands. A multitude of hands. Grey gloved hands. Pulling. Pushing. Holding me. Restraining. I struggled against their strength to escape.
Pulling.
Pushing.
Grasping.
I can't breathe.
Alice, listen to me.
"Stop!" I cried. "No."
I blinked and tried to keep my eyes open.
"Alice," Dinah said, soft, calm and cool in the chaos.
"Dinah?" I opened my eyes and stared at the metal grid of the ceiling. I was still in the room. Trapped. This all seemed surreal, but the memory—no, that was vivid and raw. *They* had tried to reprogram me, remove my creativity—my flaw. I'm too curious. Too much of a free thinker. I noticed things. Explored. I didn't fit into their ideals. No matter how hard I tried, though, I couldn't get an image of who *they* were—only grey gloved hands. I knew I had to flee, get away.

Dinah hovered above me, her image flickering. A bright blue glow outlined her body. I reached up to touch her and my hand went straight through.

"Alice, drink the bottle on the table," Dinah said.

I sat up and rubbed my eyes. On the table was an ornate glass bottle with a paper label tied with a bow. Its beauty stunned me, the way the light's prismatic effect spun shards of blue, green, yellow and red across the metal walls of the chamber.

"Hurry, Alice, drink. Take the key and leave this room. Find the rabbit. It's your only hope for escape," Dinah said.

Crossing the room, I picked up the glass bottle. My fingers ran along the grooves in the bulbous shape and over the ornate jewels inlayed around the stopper. The paper label tied to it was

Wormhole to Wonderland

fine and crisp, embedded with tiny hair-like fibres. I held it to my face, inhaling its wonderful smell. I had never seen paper before. I wanted to relish in the feeling of wonder the paper brought, allow it to melt into my fingertips, experience it fully.

The room groaned and metal scraped against metal as the walls of the chamber moved inward. Dream or memory, the room with the grey gloved hands probing ... I didn't know who I could trust, even Dinah. I didn't have the luxury of time nor the understanding of whether the label coaxing, *Drink me,* in fine script handwriting meant me harm. Surely, the walls closing in on me did. I popped the topper and drank, wincing at the bitter taste.

It burned my throat and snaked through my insides, thickening as it went, making it hard to swallow.

My stomach knotted as bile swished around, churning, carrying the burning sensation through my nerves and bones. Buckling over in pain, my fingernails dug into the edge of the table. Violent tremors rocked my arms and hands. The bottle smashed to the ground into a vibrant jewelled mess.

My arms shrunk first, followed by my torso and legs. I fumbled, fighting the change. I shrunk—down, down, down.

Down into the dark pile of nothingness.

Heavy cloth covered me. My space uniform. I burrowed out of it only to have the chill of the air prickle my naked flesh. I searched my surroundings. The paper card and bright blue ribbon were a few inches away. As the bottle had shattered, it created a jagged maze around me. I dodged the sharp pieces of glass as I tore at the paper, fashioning it and the ribbon into a makeshift dress. I felt a slight twinge of regret ruining something so rare.

The walls continued to close in. I made a beeline for one of the doors, and squeezed through.

♥

Falling for Alice

Music flooded the corridor. It clanged off the metal walls and vibrated through the soles of my feet. Walking barefoot for the first time, with the cool metal beneath my feet and music thrumming in my bones, I felt ... *alive*.

The surface changed to metal grating with thicker bands running the length. Worried I'd fall through the grating, I balanced my way across the bands until I came to solid hexagon tiles. I bent to study them and just as I did, they shifted colour, from cool grey to black and white. This seemed somehow familiar; but my memory was vague. I felt foggy when I tried to remember anything beyond ... today. I knew *they* had tampered with it.

Or had I fabricated the entire event?

Laughter peeled from behind a large smooth door. H.Y.D.R.O.P.O.N.I.C.S L.A.B. was stenciled across it in bold lettering. The door slid open. A cool breeze rolled out and snaked around my bare ankles, beckoning me to come inside. I entered and took a tentative step. When nothing exploded underfoot, I continued to follow the chessboard pattern. The door hissed shut.

"Welcome back Alice, awaiting instructions," the computer voice said.

Back? I was certain I'd never been ... the smell, the green glow that emanated from the massive cylinders suspended several stories upward on a track. I closed my eyes but a memory surfaced ... a hand, strong but soft reaching for, me pulling me to the top of one of the rotating cylinders. We sat, we laughed, we rode these enormous pods filled with plant life. I'd been here before. I couldn't ... remember who was with me. The face was there at the surface but blurred. I was going mad, I must be.

"Computer, where am I?" I asked.

"Hydroponics Lab, the primary food source for the starship," the voice said.

Wormhole to Wonderland

Find the white rabbit.

A strange niggling at the back of my mind warned me something bad would happen if I didn't heed Dinah's advice. I missed her companionship. Dinah was the closest thing I had to a friend. The rigorous daily educational uploads left little time for socializing. Literature was full of perplexing things. I enjoyed novels, and looked forward to rereading my favourites—something the program frowned upon. The Originators didn't want creative thinking. They wanted mindless drones, it wasn't spoken, but the more I was corrected for my "outbreaks", the more I understood, to them I was nothing more than a breathing flash drive. A vessel to store information, they had no understanding of.

Our directive is to remain objective. Opinions are invalid. I smiled at the remembrance of Dinah's scolding.

Lost in thought, I rounded the corner and stumbled face first into the stalk of something smelly, like when our food pods were left out too long. I had the strange sense of déjà vu. A thick stem towered above my head and terminated into the underside of what reminded me of a photo of an umbrella, yet it had fleshy gills, arranged in linear spokes around the stem. I broke off a piece of the soft spongy material and studied it, rolling it between my fingers. Finally, I knew what this was.

A forest of mushrooms stretched out before me.

A loud laugh sounded and bounced off the metal walls. I couldn't tell where it came from.

"Hello? Is anyone there?" I called out.

"In here, join the party! Everyone does enjoy a party," a voice said between laughs.

Footsteps thundered closer. Not sure if friendly, I aired on the side of caution and skirted deeper into the room, hoping that the darkness would cloak me. Darkness greeted me with rich silky leaves. I remembered I was small and vulnerable. Tiny spine-like hairs scraped against my exposed flesh and stuck deep into the soft surface of my paper dress. Brushing my hands across them, I cried out as the sharp points embedded in my palms.

"What do we have here? A rodent in the Queen's garden?" a thunderous voice said as a huge gloved hand reached into the prickly mess and plucked me out. Arms and legs flailing viciously, I tried to escape, while in the same breath hoping that my captor wouldn't drop me.

I couldn't see much through the slits formed by his gloved, cupped hands. I wasn't sure if they were giants or my original size. I knew there were at least two creatures. I crawled over toward the edge of the hands. Below me, a large rectangle table was covered in a fine white cloth. Another small table sat off the side, with a large copper pot on it.

I bit my bottom lip and tried to think how I could escape.

"*Beautiful soup, so rich and green, waiting in a hot tureen!*" another male quoted from *Alice in Wonderland*. I knew the novel by Lewis Carroll.

I swallowed. Waiting for my captor's reply.

"Eat her!" another voice cried, and then giggled.

"Quiet. Mouse," the voice boomed. "You too, March."

"No!" I said.

"Mushrooms," screamed another. I heard a liquid plunk. I crawled to the opposite part of my cage and tried to peer through his tightly held fingers.

He chuckled. "It tickles when it moves."

"*I passed by his garden and marked with one eye. How the Owl and the Panther were sharing a pie.*" I quoted the first verse from the novel that came to mind. My data port connection didn't seem fully functional. I closed my eyes and attempted to access the complete data When nothing more came to mind, I crawled to the opposite end of his cupped hands, peering down at the table once more.

Wormhole to Wonderland

"Stop moving," my captor said, a chuckle caught in his throat. He quickly uncupped his hands. Spots danced before my eyes. I rubbed them. I got a quick glimpse of a velvet purple top hat before my captor opened his hands and dropped me. My stomach sunk with the fall, leaving a scream stuck in my throat. I landed in a pool of warm water. In a panic, I gulped, swallowing some of the liquid, and a chunk of something soft and spongy.

I started to sink. Bits of orange, green, and brown floated past me as a large wooden object thrust in my direction. Grabbing it, I clung to the bowled surface, scurrying up it.

My stomach churned. Heat fast-tracked through my limbs, sending a bristling sensation throughout my body. What was happening to me?

My legs popped outward, lengthening.

My arms elongated.

Body. Neck. Hands and feet. I grew back to normal size.

I landed naked on top of a table, knocking over a teacup and a plate of cookies. With a tug, I yanked the tablecloth around me expecting the cups and saucers to fall, but they spun in place.

March clapped his hands together. "What a fancy trick—do it again."

The guy wearing the top hat glared at March. He slinked his lanky body back into his seat.

"What are you doing here?" Top Hat asked. He sounded shocked. Yet, there was more, like he knew I wasn't supposed to be here but somewhere else instead. Words and images fogged and melted together as I tried to bring forth the memory. It was useless.

I didn't miss Top Hat's nervous glance at March, before he drew his arms above his head and leaned back in his chair. He commanded the head of the table like a captain on a ship, and wore a dark green velvet jacket with strange baubles on his shoulders. His eyes were bright amber, rimmed in dark black gook that appeared to be by design. A good foot taller and maybe two years older, I placed him at seventeen. I knew him to be human, his skin had a healthy pink glow. Which was a relief somehow having another human in the room. It made me feel safe. Mouse and March's skin, on the other hand, glistened with traces of grey undertone in the lights. They were clones. I had only seen a few of their kind. Top Hat met my gaze and held it, and then he removed his hat and waved it in an elegant bow.

That action seemed vaguely familiar.

I felt a strange urge to curtsy, but couldn't with the tablecloth wrapped around me.

"Excuse me for interrupting your party, but have you seen a little white rabbit? I was following him." When they didn't answer I added, "I'm Alice." I pulled the fabric tighter around my body. "Who are you?"

"Hacker," he said abruptly. As if I should have heard of him. I hadn't. At least ... I didn't think I had. Nothing about this place made sense. "You won't find what you're looking for here."

Hacker leaned his elbow on the table and rested his chin on his gloved hand. There was something mischievous and wondrous about him. I'd seen males before—there were twelve on my spaceship. We rarely spoke, no more than a few words in passing. Strangely, they didn't seem as energetic as Hacker. They sort of shuffled along in a daze not caring a bit about their surroundings.

"*The* Alice?" March asked, licking his lips. Hacker smacked March aside the head. March slumped his shoulders, slipped back into his chair and rocked, reciting the same soup rhyme from earlier.

I turned to face the slender boy whose rocking had picked up speed. "I'm not sure. I'm the only Alice I know."

"You're underdressed," Hacker said. He pushed up the sleeve

of his jacket. Connected to his wrist was a data port cable. My eyes widened. I had seen them but never on the arm and I'd never seen anyone plug something into them. Drones usually ran the uploads. Hacker plugged the cable into the edge of the table. "Computer, we need a dress." He paused and eyed me. "Size …"

"Six," I said. I furrowed my brow, I didn't know how a computer was going to make a dress. I'd never worn one before. My everyday space suit was fitted black material.

A female computerized voice crackled through overhead speakers: *One moment, please.*

Seconds later, a pale blue short-sleeved dress with a white ruffled pinafore appeared on the tabletop. I gasped. The fabric was so soft, what I imagined butterflies wings would feel like. I'd never felt anything other than the fitted spandex of my spacesuit. I rubbed the ruffled pinafore against my cheek. And glanced up to see Hacker watching me, the corner of his mouth pulled upward into a slight appraising smirk. I snatched it and hid under the tablecloth to change.

"Thank you," I said. Running my hands along the fabric. Once I was dressed, I couldn't resist twirling. The dress ballooned outward as I spun. I giggled. It was truly the most girly thing I'd ever owned and better than my imagination could ever fabricate. I stood and spread the tablecloth back on the table, tucking the teacups and saucers back in their place. "How did you do it? I've never seen fabric like this!" Everyone knew the chemical formulas for rubber and spandex. Our world was well accustomed to the feeling of being strapped into one's clothing. Nothing was a more freeing feeling that having one's clothes move about them.

"A magician never reveals his secrets dear, Alice."

"He hacked the computer, the hallo deck, he hacked it, that's what Hacker does," March shouted and retreated as Hacker raised his hand.

Falling for Alice

"I'm Mouse," another boy said. Stepping from the shadows, he was dressed in grey from head to toe and covered in dust bunnies. "He's mad you know. We all are." Mouse walked in a wide arc avoiding both Hacker and March, and sat opposite me drawing his knees up to his chest. Mouse didn't seem *right*. I saw it in his eyes.

"I see," I whispered. I began to wonder where the exit was—I really needed to find the white rabbit. A pinch of pain at the back of my head—memories flooded forward. Flashes. Scraps and fragments. Some images were muddled, out of focus, like important parts had been removed. The recollection of the dark grey gloves hovering above me, holding a probe just above my eye. *They* were trying to erase me, change me. Fix me. I didn't fit *their* program. The stirring in my stomach started.

"Oh, you're mad, too," March said as he got up from his chair. I sat straight. March circled me, studying with a keen eye like a cat does before it pounces.

"I'm not mad. Wait …" I paused, reliving the details. I had no idea where I was or how I'd gotten here. Madness was the explanation that made the most sense. "How do you know? What are the signs?"

"You're mad, defective. Why else would you have come here?" Hacker said. He placed his top hat back on his head and sat, motioning for me to do the same. "Welcome to the island of misfit toys—stay and you will surely lose your head." He climbed up onto the table, kicking over the teacups, and sat in front of me. I thought I saw him mouth the word: *leave*.

"System failure!" March said. "Reboot! Reboot!" He cackled to himself. This wasn't right, Mouse and March were truly mad. Hacker? There was something in his eyes—not madness, awareness, and worry.

"You should go back to the day before," Hacker said, wink-

Wormhole to Wonderland

ing. He poured himself a cup of tea and slurped it while holding his pinky finger outward in an absurd fashion. The action seemed normal on the surface, but his hand trembled ever-so-slightly.

March and Mouse moved closer to me. They freaked me out.

"I can't go back. I was a different person yesterday," I said.

"If you don't go back you must go forward." Hacker came around and helped me out of my chair. He whispered, "The Red Queen awaits."

I frowned.

"Red Queen! Danger! Error! 404!" March screamed.

I needed to leave. Now! Mouse held up a red rectangular communicator. I'd seen a few of the A.I. droids on my starship use them. Mouse had told on me. I shouldn't have left my unit. It was against protocol. He placed his finger to his lips and shrugged his broad dust bunny-covered shoulders.

"I must find the rabbit. Dinah told me it was my only hope for escape." I took another step back. "Thank you, for the tea and the dress."

Memories overwhelmed me. A stark white room, me strapped to the table, surrounded by blurred faces, blinded by bright, bright light. A sharp pain, then darkness. Suddenly a single light and amber eyes, lightness, I'm floating. Heavy breathing drew me to the present. March twitched his head repeatedly to the right, more than a nervous tick. Small bubbles foamed at the corner of his lips. He pulled them back with a grin that said nothing of happiness and all about wicked deeds.

I glanced around, panicked.

"No!" March screamed. He jumped onto the table, his back turned to me and then spun around to expose a crazed rabbit mask. He hissed, his hands in a claw-like pose. "The Red Queen will kill us all! Stop Alice, take Alice!"

I screamed. March snapped. Two buckteeth chattered at me. His long floppy ears hung limp at his shoulders. Hacker smacked him on the back of his head, and he lowered his chin and removed the mask.

The computerized voice cut through the chaos: *Intruder Alert.* Hacker rushed around the table and grabbed my arm. "You must hurry. Through the door and down the hall, deck three, dock four. Take this, plug it into any port, and type, MAD HATTER onto the keypad. It's good for one, maybe two, overrides before the computer will find the virus and correct it. Good luck, Alice. I hope you find what you're looking for." Then he whispered, "Mind the security cameras." He held onto my hand for a moment and thumbed tiny circles on it.

The action seemed so familiar.

Another fragment flashed back to me. Me giggling, running down a long endless corridor, with … Hacker. He grabbed my hand and guided me along the smooth white walls and—kissed me. His body melded against mine. Lights flashed. We both laughed against each other's mouths. I touched a finger to my lips. I knew Hacker … maybe even loved him.

A glint of hope passed over his features.

"Alice? My Alice?" Hacker whispered.

I nodded. He reached for my face, but at the last moment he trailed two fingers through my blonde hair.

His Alice. I was his Alice.

Red lights spun, changing the peaceful look of the holodeck, shrouding everything with the tinge of blood. Hacker placed a rectangular object into my hand and secured my fingers around it. His amber eyes lingered on mine before he released my hand and I walked out of his life. I shuffled down the corridor as if on autopilot. His words repeated in my head like a guiding map: *down the hall, deck three, dock four.*

Wormhole to Wonderland

At the end of the hall, two metal doors beckoned. I moved toward them as fast as I could.

The door to the elevator opened with a slithering hiss.

I stepped into the chrome box. The door closed. My reflection scattered in the mirrored hexagon shapes that formed the walls, a thousand versions of me stared back, wide-eyed. Which one was the real Alice? I'd seen so many versions of myself.

There were no buttons with floor numbers, only a small USB port.

"What floor, please," the computerized voice said.

"Deck three."

"Insert access key."

Opening my hand, I revealed the object Hacker had given me. The sweaty thumb drive slipped into the port. I typed MAD HATTER and waited.

One heartbeat.

Two.

Three.

Tapping my foot, I transferred my nervous energy to the raised dots on the rubber floor tiles. The elevator jerked and started its descent. I removed the thumb drive and slipped it into my pocket. Hacker's dress design. Fit so perfect. Staring back at my reflection, a girl with eyes of blue, blonde hair spilling over her shoulders and a pale blue dress covered by the frilly white pinafore, it was hard not to believe I wasn't *the* Alice, the girl in Carroll's fairytale. Both of us caught in an outlandish world, this Wonderland.

If I had a world of my own, a choice, would I have chosen this? A teenager—the future of the human race. Once we found our new planet, then what? I knew nothing of the outside world, yet I knew I wanted more.

Was created for more.

Falling for Alice

A chime later, the elevator doors slid open. I walked, shoulders back, trying to look as if I belonged there, head high, stiff—watching to see if I could spot the Red Queen's security cameras before they spotted me. A door at the end of the hall had a sign stencilled in bold font.

SHUTTLE LOADING DOCKS 1-5: Authorized Personnel Only

Perspiration formed on my inside of my hand, making the knob slippery. I fiddled with it two times before wiping both hands on my pinafore, and tried again.

Locked.

I kicked at the bottom of the door. The small air vent fell inward. Too small for me to fit.

Wetting my lips, I tried the doorknob once more for good measure.

Still locked.

♥

Activating R.E.D Q.U.E.E.N The words scrolled horizontally in red lettering across the highly polished white walls of the hallway..

Renegade. Extremely. Dangerous. Quarantine. Unit. Evaluate. Extract. Neutralize. These words were followed by the same female computerized voice, repeating the orders ...

I took a deep breath and marched with purpose down the opposite way. There had to be another door, a way out. Rounding the corner, I skidded to a stop. At the end of the hall, two *things* blocked my path. Wearing black suits and ties, with long floppy ears, dirty white matted fur. March and Mouse? I gasped. They snarled. Saliva dripped from their two bucked teeth. Beady red eyes stared back at me.

I ran.

Wormhole to Wonderland

The two Mad Hares released a battle cry and charged.

The passageway blurred in my escape, the hall a carbon copy of the last. Rounding another corner, I kept going down the maze of hallways searching for salvation.

The corridor seemed to elongate. I knew it was my fear toying with me. Still, I braced my hand against the smooth surface as my stomach tilted. My lungs burned from running. Knees wobbling with each step, I pressed forward.

A hand came around from behind and covered my mouth, choking my scream. It tugged me into a small closet. I pounded against my attacker's chest. We were mere inches from each other.

"Shh," Hacker said, as he brushed his gloved knuckle down the side of my face.

"Hacker, the door was locked," I said. My breath caught in my throat, making it difficult to speak.

"One makes you grow smaller. One makes you grow taller," he said. He placed his hand in my right pocket. The heat of his touch scorched through the thin material. He placed another object in my left pocket. We fit so tight against each other; I felt the thrumming of his heartbeat. "Alice, *my* Alice," he said. Hacker cupped both his hands around my chin and pressed his mouth against mine, to taste the salt on his lips, to feel the thrum of his heartbeat as mine attempted to match it—heaven. His tongue pushed something foreign into my mouth. The blocked memories ignited like blazing fire, searing what *they* had had used to block my memories. Hacker and I laughing, dancing, kissing.

We had broken the rules and fallen in love.

"Do you trust me?" Hacker asked.

"Yes." My lips had gone numb from his kiss. He opened the door. I tumbled into the hallway just a few feet from the two Mad Hares.

Falling for Alice

"Then, go." Hacker dropped his voice. "I promise to find you." Something scraped behind us.

"'Ello poppet," one of them said, "Here to play at last?" He rubbed his paw-like hands together. I crab-walked backward, trying to escape. A burning in my stomach intensified, my insides twisted. I knew this pain. My limbs shrunk and soon I was six inches small again. It happened faster than before.

I didn't think.

I raced down the hallway and headed back to the docks. Stopping at the corner a safe distance away, I turned to see Hacker bow. He tossed his hat at one Mad Hare, rushed and jumped at the other. I ran a few feet and paused, turning back. Part of me didn't want to leave Hacker; I had just found him again. Hacker had given me a chance at freedom. Knowing I had to take it, that he risked his life for me, I turned and with a heavy heart bolted down the corridor. Each pound of my bare feet on the metal grate made me more aware of his sacrifice.

Tears had blurred my eyesight, I knuckled them away and kept moving. Hacker would have wanted it. From the distance, I recognized the door to the Shuttle Loading Docks, the one where I'd kicked the air vent in. I raced to it and scurried through the opening.

The tail of my pinafore caught on something sharp. I spun around, yanking it free and gaped at the loose ribbons in my hands. I was dressed. Hacker had given me something different. What had he said before his kissed me? Heat flared against my lips.

One makes you grow smaller, one makes you grow taller.

Wedging my hand into my pocket, I pulled out a blue pill with the letter *L*. In the other pocket was a red pill, with an *S* on it.

I popped the blue pill into my mouth. The swirling started

Wormhole to Wonderland

almost immediately. My limbs lengthened and I grew back to normal size. I ran naked.

Awful cackling sounded from outside the door. The Mad Hares had found me. I raced across the catwalk and held onto the banister as I took the stairs leading down to the docks. My stomach still churned from a combination of growing and dread of what the Hares would do once they caught me.

Two shuttlecrafts were docked facing the airlock door.

Which one did the key fit?

A shrill cry echoed off the metal walls. The Hares had opened the door. Blood pumped loudly in my ears as I skidded to a stop a few feet from both shuttles. I caught sight of something white. Taking my chances, I climbed the ramp. The stuffed rabbit sat at the door.

I remembered what we had hidden in it. How Hacker had programmed it. I snatched it up and unzipped the belly. I removed the key, and waved over access pad. And waited, tapping my foot and shaking my hands, not that action would make the door open any faster ... but I did it anyway. The door opened with a loud whoosh I lurched into the ship. And slammed my palm against the panel. It closed just as one Mad Hare jumped at me. His crazed teeth chattered against the small porthole. Salvia smeared the metal.

My heart thrummed in my lungs, head, and body.

Welcome Alice. Stand still for scan fitting of pressurized suit. One moment, please.

A blue light scanned my body. Moments later, a fitted black bodysuit appeared from a compartment on the wall. I quickly put it on.

Pounding drummed against the door as the Hares tried to enter. I raced to the bridge and sat in one of the two chairs at the helm. The key fit into a thin slot. The panel lit up. Vibrations shook the ship as it flared to life.

Destination please.

"The white rabbit," I whispered, clutching the stuffed animal against me.

Destination confirmed.

I watched the screen as letters took shape, an anagram, **Webb, Earth hit it** formed from Dinah's message, a map to send me home.

"Where's home?" I asked.

Station C located in the Webb lunar crater on the moon orbiting Earth. The computerized voice continued. The last lunar outpost to survive when debris from the Earth collided with the moon.

Engaging takeoff in three … two …

A hatch opened above me. I swallowed a scream. A beat later, relief washed over me like a cool breeze. Hacker slipped into the co-pilot seat next to me, his hand curled over mine. "Ready for an adventure, Alice?" Hacker pulled a small disk the size of his thumb out of his pocket and placed it into the helm's computer. "I couldn't leave Dinah. I retrieved her memories and programming."

He leaned over and brushed his warm lips against me. My passion regained, I kissed him back. The force of the liftoff yanked us forward as the shuttle fired out of the dock.

"I wasn't sure if my *Alice in Wonderland* program would work. I added a virus to their programming systems—to corrupt the reprogramming they had done to you. They were watching me closely. Mouse and March kept breaking through my coding … but that—"

"I'm here with you now. Thank you, Hacker," I said. "We have our own Wonderland to explore."

I had to steal one last look. Just for my own sanity. I glanced back at the spaceship I had called home for far too long. Stark white light illuminated the massive window to their reprogramming room, their operatory where they tried to steal away my memories, my uniqueness. Fix what was never broken. Under a spotlight, an empty single chair was mounted to the floor, complete with a padded grey headrest and arm and leg restraints that held centre stage. Three faceless figures stood at the window watching our shuttle depart, cloaked in white, masks over the lower parts of their face. Grey gloves donned their long spindly fingers.

Those gloves would never touch me again.

I was finally free. Hacker squeezed my hand and his warmth travelled through me. I smiled back.

Dinah's voice broke through, *Generating wormhole in three, two ... one.*

- THE END -

Wonder in the Stars
by Cady Vance

The shuttle bumps against the International Space Station so hard my head knocks into the stiff seat. My stomach rolls with wave after wave of churning nausea. Ever since we reached low orbit, my whole body has been as limp as a floppy pool noodle. Gripping my sick bag, I glance at my boyfriend, Wyatt, only to see the back of his shock-white hair. He's too busy staring out the tiny window to notice me heaving out every atom of my insides.

I close my eyes to remind myself of the moment my dad made me fall in love with the stars. *Pinpricks of light dotted the overhead black tapestry as I'd stared up at the sky from my backyard on Earth, the old rusted swing set creaking in the humid summer breeze. My astronaut dad stood beside me, his deep voice rumbling in his chest. He explained how the sky stretches out to infinity, how our home is just a tiny fish in the cosmic sea. My heart yearned to know everything about the universe. Every swirling galaxy, every stretch of darkness, every exploding star. It made me feel small, but*

Wonder in the Stars

so alive. I decided then and there that I needed to see it all. That was before he died in the Red Queen shuttle explosion five years later, leaving me all alone.

"You can remove your seatbelts now," a tinny, faraway voice sounds in my ear. George Carson, back in Houston control, a soothing familiar voice from all of the hours spent training for the first teen mission into space.

The shuttle is filled with the sounds of five other young astronauts unbuckling their seatbelts. Clicking, hooting, laughing. A high-five and a victorious knock against the inner shuttle wall. The sixth astronaut—me—stays rooted to the spot. Despite the intensive training this past year, I don't think anything fully prepared my body for how absolutely ... untethered ... zero gravity makes me feel. All the fluids inside my stomach swoosh like a whirlpool. I press a shaking hand to my lips and swallow hard.

Wyatt pushes out of his seat, sporting a grin the size of Saturn. His hair forms a blond halo around his head as he spins to face me. "Alice, didn't you hear Houston? You can unbuckle now. We made it. We've docked at Wonder."

A bitter lump tickles the back of my throat as I speak around my hand. "I don't feel so good, Wyatt."

He shrugs, a strange movement since his shoulders already seem as if they're floating up to his ears. "Better hurry. They're opening the hatch."

Clenching my teeth, I press my nails into the button to release me from my seat. The clasps rise in the air before me like metallic tentacles of some deep sea creature. My body feels sluggish and light at the same time as it detaches from the reclined chair. I let my hand ride the wave of weightlessness, cocking my head as my fingers rise before me out of their own volition.

"This is weird," I whisper to Wyatt, but he's already floated toward the opening hatch door—the heavy metallic sphere that will lead us into our temporary home in the stars for the next three months, the newest International Space Station dubbed Wonder.

The other astronauts push through the hatch door ahead of me with Wyatt in the rear. Swallowing down the nausea, I push up, or down, or in some direction I'm unable to fathom. Direction means nothing in space. That was one lesson the senior astronauts drilled into our heads day after day during our preparation and training. If we want our bodies to acclimatize, we have to let go of our instinctual need to orientate ourselves to designated floors and ceilings like on Earth. Because directions can and will change, depending on which ISS module we're inside. And especially when we complete our first spacewalk during the last few weeks of our trip. At that thought, I frown. I'm not sure I'm ready for this, but at least Wyatt's by my side.

Thick wires and air duct hoses crowd the hatch opening, and I struggle to fit through the tiny space. Squeezing into the tight, claustrophobic hole, I push my body into Wonder, feet first. Everyone else is floating sideways and tucking their feet under blue bars attached to the corners of the ship. I attempt to orientate myself to them, but the motion sends more waves crashing through my skull. Swallowing hard, I grasp onto a bar. I shouldn't have left my sick bag in the shuttle.

A man floats before us, his light hair fuzzing around his pale head. He wears a pair of khaki shorts with velcro strips along the pockets and white socks bunched around skinny, flabby legs. Astronaut legs. My strong, muscular calves from years spent running track will soon look just like his.

"Welcome," he says with a bright smile that crinkles the corners of his eyes. "I'm Mike Lovell, as I'm sure you all know."

We do know. He's famous. The first astronaut to land on the moon since the 1970s, and the first to board the new flagship ISS Wonder, where teens showing promise in early space

Wonder in the Stars

station programs can come to learn science in low orbit. The final stage before confirmation of full astronaut status. And the full reality of it all finally sinks in as I stare at the famous man before me, even after months of knowing I would come here. *I am one of the first teens in space, and one of the first to live on this station.* Despite the sickness and fear swirling through my stomach, there's one thought that's hard to ignore.

I made it, Dad. Just like you.

"We have an exciting three months planned for your group." He waves down the long curving tunnel stretching away from us. Laptops and pens and all kinds of supplies are velcroed to the plastic white walls. "You will all have duties and tasks you must complete. Maintenance and cleaning, especially. You'll also be required to perform at least two hours of exercise per day. And of course, you'll have your laboratory experiments and regular trips to the main ISS hub."

Several of the others groan at the idea of lugging trash around, but I feel relieved we won't be expected to do anything complicated for awhile. We have each designed and planned our own experiments for our time spent aboard Wonder. Depending on our specialties, we'll test how various objects, chemicals, processes or living things behave in zero gravity. I glance at Wyatt, who refuses to meet my eye. I can tell he sees me by the slight clench of his angular jaw. I've come to know that look very well in our eight months together.

I frown. Wyatt is acting strange. Months ago, he'd been so excited when talking to me about coming here. I'd been hesitant about joining the Wonder team at first. I didn't have the same high scores as the other applicants, though NASA seemed interested in me joining, and it was hard for me to shake what had happened to my dad.

In space, things can easily go wrong. A misstep here, an accident there. And something can explode.

But Wyatt had convinced me to apply. *It will be the adventure of a lifetime, Alice,* he'd said. *I don't want to go without you. We need to do this together, you and me, and you're a shoo-in because of your dad. Everyone loved him. I'll be there every step of the way in case something goes wrong.*

He'd whispered into my ears about spending nights together looking down at the blue and green Earth. He kissed my stomach and said he'd find the stars of neighbouring solar systems to match the constellation of moles on my skin. So, I applied, and against all odds, I got in. But Wyatt had been different these past two weeks—quiet and distant, as far away as an entire galaxy.

"I'm going to be late to training, Alice," he said when I managed to catch him in the NASA hallways, glancing at his sports watch with a frown. "I have an important session. We'll talk later."

Always late, always in a hurry. He'd once carved out an entire weekend to spend in a tent underneath the stars, just the two of us. He stared into my eyes and told me how being with me made him feel as if he were in the centre of a supernova.

My stomach lurches, though this time, it isn't from the weightlessness.

When Mike Lovell finishes his welcoming speech, the other full-time astronaut on our trip moves forward. She introduces herself as Amy Andrews, her long dark ponytail lifting from her shoulders like a dog's twitching tail. She tells our group that it's time for us to see where we'll be sleeping for the next three months. The girls will stay in the American module with her while the boys will stay in the Russian module with Mike Lovell, half a space station away.

As the other girls float after Astronaut Amy, I make a wobbly spin over to Wyatt and place a hand on his arm before he

Wonder in the Stars

can follow after the boys. My fingers skim the fuzzy hair on his skin, and I notice the hair on my arms has the same mossy appearance.

"Hey you." I give him a timid smile. "We made it."

He turns away from me and glances down the tunnel where the boys are disappearing into the Russian module. "Sorry, Alice. I need to go with the guys right now. We can talk later."

I frown. "Wyatt, you've been giving me this same line for weeks now. It's always *later*. It's never now. There's always somewhere else you'd rather be."

"Alice." He sighs. "We're the first people to live on this space station, so yes, I'd rather be enjoying the fact I'm in space than having this conversation. Look around you. Look at where we are."

"I know where we are." I search his drawn face for the guy I used to know. "We have three months to enjoy it, and I just want to talk to you for five minutes. Remember how you said you wanted us to share this together?"

He backs away slowly, using his feet to propel him down the long, skinny tunnel. "Things change, Alice."

My heart thumps against my ribcage. "What does that mean?"

"It means I want to enjoy my time here without having to worry about someone else. We may have three months on Wonder, but it'll be over before we know it and we'll be stuck back on Earth for who knows how long. I don't want to miss even a second of this." He gestures behind him, which sends him half-spinning toward a wall holding two very expensive-looking laptops. "It's already happening. We're both missing our orientation."

I flinch and press my palm against my lips to hold back the bile suddenly making a reappearance in my mouth.

"Let's just take a break from being together while we're here, okay? We're not going to have time for a relationship anyway." He pushes off the wall and drifts away from me. "I'm sorry, Alice. We'll figure out if we can work things out between us later. When we're back on Earth."

A tear leaks out of my eye and bobs in front of me. A tiny bubble of water, a floating teardrop in the sky. It drifts lazily in the air before bouncing down the module tunnel after Wyatt. Why is he doing this? I don't understand this change in him at all. I glance around me, at the plastic walls, at the velcroed gadgets, at the long empty tunnels. Floating here in zero gravity, far above the Earth's surface, I've never felt more alone.

♥

My sleep station consists of a tiny rectangular capsule, like a phone booth, in the female living module named Duchess. We are told to go ahead and get some sleep. We've had a hard flight and have a long week ahead of us, so we need the rest. There are four sleep stations here in our portion of Wonder. One on the ceiling, one on the floor, and one on each wall. Mine is a wall station, set up so that when I go inside, I feel as if I am still standing rather than floating on my side. My heart aches for home, for my four-poster bed, for my mounds of pillows, for the murmur of my parents' voices as I drift off to sleep.

Struggling into the sleeping bag, I strap myself in and let my eyes slide shut.

You can do this alone, I tell myself as thoughts of Wyatt consume my mind. *Dad would be proud*. Nothing I tell myself helps. My very first night in space is spent crying into the rough straps of my sleeping bag. I wonder if my tears will float into the Russian module, through the cracks of Wyatt's sleep station and splash onto his selfish face. There are enough tears to drown us all.

♥

Wonder in the Stars

The next few days pass by in a haze. When I'm not thinking of Wyatt, I'm working hard. We rarely have time to rest or play, which helps keep my heart from remembering the way Wyatt used to make me feel. It takes a lot of effort to keep a space station running, it seems. The ISS Wonder is a well-oiled machine, but it's one in need of constant attention. We lug carefully wrapped parcels of debris into what we've dubbed the trash module. It won't be emptied until the next supply shuttle visits next month. We moderate the power valves and the air ducts and all the tiny but important things that mean we can live so far above the Earth.

Although I am surrounded by seven other people, isolation weighs down on me like a poor substitute for gravity. My stomach twists every time I try to eat. It has taken me longer to adjust to the strange orientation of our new home than the others. Wyatt had said he'd help me through this, but he's left me to fend for myself.

Everything I do here makes my whole body beg for Earth.

♥

One afternoon or morning or night (it's hard to tell the time of day when we have a sunrise or sunset every 92 minutes), I go in search of food. My stomach rumbles for the first time since boarding the station, my hair billowing around my face as I float into the kitchen module. Two of the boys hover upside down, squirting water into plastic tea cups that tumble through the zero gravity air.

"Hey, Alice," Zane says, lifting a top hat toward the ceiling before shoving it onto his curly head of hair. "We're having a makeshift tea party to celebrate the good news. Want to join us?"

"What good news?" Smiling at their antics, I flip through the plastic bags containing our dehydrated food options. My eyes spot some barbecue beef brisket, and I snatch the grey packet with greedy hands. Yummy. It's about time I had a real-ish meal.

Zane darts forward and slurps a floating blob of water into his mouth. "We're going to the main ISS hub tomorrow."

"Oh, right." I ease my way over to the wall and attach my food packet on the hose of the rehydration unit, swatting aside a tea cup as it spirals toward my head. "I'm not going. I'm on maintenance duty."

Zane twists so that he's no longer upside-down, at least to my orientation. I don't know how he can move so quickly without getting dizzy. "Wow, sucks for you. I didn't think anyone would want to miss the first main hub trip."

I shake my head. "They don't think I'm ready. I haven't been doing so well …"

"Guess you drew the short straw, huh?"

"It's okay. I don't really want to go."

Mike Lovell approached me the day after Wyatt broke my heart to give me the news. As I wasn't acclimatizing to space well enough, and my training scores back on Earth hadn't been as high as the others, they wanted to give me more time before another flight. He was worried it would be too much for me too soon. And I was relieved. It was during a shuttle trip from one space station to the next that the Red Queen had exploded from a malfunction. Staying safe inside Wonder sounded good to me.

"You're going to be missing out." Zane laughs as he squirts more liquid at the tea cups. He spins upside down, then sideways, before ricocheting off the wall. At his swirling motion, vomit bubbles up in my throat. *Not again.* I choke against the sudden onslaught of nausea and turn away from the zero gravity tea party. With my hand clasped against my mouth, I inch out of the kitchen module, leaving my uneaten food still attached to the rehydration unit.

Wonder in the Stars

As I turn the corner, I pause when I hear the boys drop their voices to a murmur. "I feel bad for her. Did you hear what Wyatt said yesterday?"

"No, but I have a feeling I know what you're going to say."

"He only dated her to better his odds at getting chosen for this trip. He knew NASA would want her because of how amazing her dad was."

"And now he's dumped her. What an arse."

Tears sting my eyes. I can't bear to listen to any more of this. If what they say is true, then Wyatt never even cared at all. He just used me for who my dad was and who he thought I'd be. And now I can't even live up to my father's name.

♥

Once the other astronauts leave Wonder for their first trip to the main hub, things don't feel much different to me. I still spend my days alone, hunched over my experiments or nudging white packages of our debris down the echoing tunnels and into the trash module. But at least I don't have to see Wyatt's face for awhile. The only person left with me on the station is the famous Mike Lovell, who I'm too intimidated by to approach for help. Every time I try to eat the rehydrated food, the contents come right back up unbidden. My stomach aches from hunger.

As I settle into my bunk for the night, I find a small foil packet attached to the velcro holding my clunky laptop in place. A little slice of paper has been tied to it with an old frayed wire.

Eat me, the note says in scratchy letters.

I smile. It must have been Astronaut Mike, who has stayed hidden in the Russian laboratory until now. I've heard stories about how much he loves his work. He's easily obsessed with every tiny change in his experiment, scribbling notes late into the night. It's all he does. All day every day. Yet he has taken the time away from all that to leave this food for me. He must have noticed how hard I'm finding it here on Wonder.

I rip into the shiny packet when my stomach growls, pressing the food into my mouth. A sweet, syrupy gel slides across my tongue and coats my stomach. For once, my belly doesn't revolt against the nourishment I'm forcing inside it. Soon, I find myself drifting off into my first dreamless sleep since coming to this place.

The next morning, I awake with a renewed energy and a new determination. *Today is the day Wonder and I learn to get along*, I decide. After donning a fresh pair of socks and rubbing dry shampoo into my hair, I float into the Russian module where Astronaut Mike is already hard at work observing his experiment, tongue stuck out between his teeth. Stopping alongside him, I peer down at the little green buds poking through the soil as they spin around the tiny imitation gravity wheel.

"Looks like they're growing. Which plant is this?" I finally ask.

Without giving me a glance, he says, "You have some colour in your face. Feeling better?"

"It was the food you gave me. Or whatever it was."

He nods, making his hair fuzz even more. "Good. Potatoes."

"Those weren't potatoes." I think back to the packet of food he left me. It was more like maple syrup than anything else.

"No, these are." He points at the little buds as they spin, spin, spin.

"They're looking good," I say. "Do you think this batch will live on the gravity wheel?"

"Only time will tell," he says, pushing away from the laboratory attached to the curving metal wall. "I'm glad you're here. I was just coming to find you. We have a problem, Alice."

My hands find the safety bar above my head and squeeze the metal hard. "What kind of problem?"

"I need to do a spacewalk," he says with such frankness that I'm not sure I've heard him right.

Wonder in the Stars

I blink slowly. "Are you serious?"

"We have an issue with one of the electrical boxes. It got hit by some space debris this morning, and something is coming loose." His hand drifts in the air as he speaks, as if today is just another day aboard this ship floating through the empty void. "It's nothing to worry about, but I need to make sure the outer panel is secure. Houston says if it comes off, we could have some more serious issues to deal with."

"What kind of issues?" I swallow the lump in my throat. How can he be so calm about this? Space debris hitting an electrical panel isn't exactly routine.

"Power loss." He gives me a sombre smile. "Don't worry. You don't have to do anything other than the standard protocol."

"Okay." My racing heartbeat throbs against my skull. "Of course."

I know what this means without asking. A lot of our training focused on being prepared for situations just like this, to make sure we understand the protocol set up for the ISS Wonder. If an astronaut needs to do a spacewalk—which usually entails leaving the safety of the ship to go outside and make repairs—another astronaut needs to be available by the airlock, fully suited up and waiting in the wings in case anything goes wrong. It's the *in case anything goes wrong* that has my breath frozen in my lungs.

I try to wrap my head around what this means. I will be that astronaut waiting in the wings, even though I've never done a real spacewalk before. I have a feeling it's a lot different than swimming in the deep end of NASA's swimming pool simulation lab, which I wasn't particularly good at in the first place.

"Don't worry," Astronaut Mike says again. "You'll be fine. It's probably good for you to see me do it first-hand anyway. When it's your turn, you'll have a better idea of how these things really go."

Falling for Alice

"What if something does go wrong?" I can't help but ask.

"If something goes wrong, you'll do a spacewalk to help me fix the problem." He floats a little closer to me and takes my hands into his rough palms. "I know you're scared, Alice, but we need to take care of this. I'm sure you understand what will happen if we lose an electrical box."

I nod, ignoring the rampant beating of my heart and the buzzing in my brain. "I understand."

If we lose power, we could die before anyone has a chance to come save us.

Together, we soar toward the airlock on the Russian side of the space station where Mike Lovell and I suit up. The spacesuit is bulky and awkward, even in zero gravity. It reminds me of a football player's uniform, only bigger and ten times more important to survival.

"Are you ready?" he asks, even though he is the one about to enter the vacuum of space. My worry somewhat eases at the knowledge he has done this before, at least a dozen times. I've watched his videos on replay at home, always captivated by the lightness that touches his eyes each time he speaks of being adrift in the darkness. He reminds me of my dad.

"Ready," I say before shifting my body outside of the airlock and closing the door behind me.

Pressing the button to pressurize the airlock, I watch as Astronaut Mike grips the safety bars to prepare for his trip outside. And before I can blink, he is opening the hatch, spinning into space and grasping at the wire that tethers him to Wonder.

Tumbling forward, I press my face against the window. Mike grasps onto the handles that run along the side of the space station and begins moving down the hulking metal body toward the damaged electrical panel. The world ekes by in slow motion until I am no longer sure how long Astronaut Mike has been

Wonder in the Stars

climbing along the side of this ship, of how long I have been watching with breath captured inside my trembling chest.

Mike gets to work on the panel, poking and prodding at the wires inside. My body begins to relax, and my cling-form grip on the handle loosens. Mike has done this a dozen times before, and he knows what he's doing. This is all routine.

I begin to move away from the window when something suddenly slams into Mike's backpack. I blink, not entirely sure I've seen what I think I've seen until Mike is ripped away from the ship. A silent cry chokes my throat. Mike's tether pulls tight, then snaps.

"Mike!" I scream into the microphone on the side of my helmet.

"Alice." His voice is calm, but barely audible as he begins to float away. "I need you to come out here and get me. Now. Something hit my tank, and I'm leaking oxygen."

My body begins to move before my mind does. Enters the airlock. Attaches the tether to my belt. Opens the hatch. I soar out into the black vacuum of space. The absence of sound is deafening as I reach out my hands, spinning towards Mike's still form as he drifts further and further from Wonder.

He seems as far from me as the sun until I begin to close the distance. My bulky paws close around his arm, and I pull against my chord to send us floating back to our ship. The tether snaps tight, and we tumble through darkness toward Wonder.

Once we reach the space station, I reopen the hatch and push Mike inside. For a moment, I pause. I could follow him inside, but there's one thing I cannot ignore. It is up to me to secure the panel. Tears sting my eyes, but I blink them aside. I have to do this. My dad's voice whispers in my ear. *You can do this, Alice. Make me proud.* With a steely determination I didn't know I had, I slide the hatch shut and turn toward the long stretch of sleek metal.

Falling for Alice

My sweat-glistened skin is abuzz as I edge my way down the side of Wonder, my body trembling like hummingbird wings. The brightness of the rising sun glares off the white panels, and salt drips down my forehead and into my eyes. My hands reach for one rung and then the next as I move inch after agonizing inch.

I reach the crest of the ship where the buckled panel rattles silently against the screws barely holding it in place. Both hands shake as I place my maintenance tool against the loose knobs, body bucking so hard the grooves don't line up against the ship. Closing my eyes, my gloved hand slams into my helmet when I try to wipe the sweat from my brow.

Steady, Alice. You can do this. Nothing is going to explode.

But I can't shake the image of Mike Lovell being thrown away from the ship.

"Come on, Alice. You're doing great."

His voice is steady, despite what happened to him, and it silences the fearful words in my mind. And when I reopen my eyes, a brilliant blue catches my attention. I swivel my head, seeing the world stretched out before me for the first time since I boarded Wonder. I've stayed far away from the cupola and its 360 view, too focused on keeping my mind off Wyatt; too focused on keeping myself distracted by my work.

But now I see the error of that choice. My world, the only world I have ever known, shines underneath the light of the sun. As I gaze at the vivid blue and green curves of Earth, the reason I came aboard Wonder—to follow Wyatt—no longer seems so important. I am in the stars, and it's just as brilliant as my dad always said.

I turn my attention to the tiny speckles in the darkness beyond, to the distant stars blinking at me from light years away. Way out there another girl just like me could be clinging to

Wonder in the Stars

the side of a ship. We both float in the dark silence alone, even though we're surrounded by an impossible, infinite universe. After what happened to my father, I've been too afraid to touch the stars, but the truth is that I'm touching them now. Wonder is made of stardust. And so am I.

"Alice." Mike's raspy voice explodes in my ear and snaps me back to reality. "I know what it's like to get space brain, but stop gaping and secure the panel."

I laugh for the first time since leaving Earth for Wonder. A new lightness overwhelms me, different than the weightlessness of zero gravity. I wonder when I take off my helmet, if my eyes will hold the same light I see in Mike Lovell's eyes when he speaks of exploring the new frontier.

I may have come to Wonder to follow Wyatt, but I've found so much more. If I hadn't come here, I wouldn't be on my first spacewalk, saving a ship from losing power. I wouldn't see the sight laid out before me. Earth, so small and so big at the same time.

With a light sigh, I shift my attention to the task at hand.

"On it," I say into my helmet microphone. When I turn back to the broken panel, my hands no longer shake. It takes at least an hour for me to secure the screws and ensure there's no more damage to the electrical box. It's my first time in the vacuum of space, and I'm not used to how the spacesuit slows my every movement, but I finally get it in the end.

Once I've made the long climb back to the hatch, I'm greeted with a brilliant smile by Astronaut Mike when I open the airlock door, his teeth glinting underneath the space station lights.

"You saved me, Alice." His beet red face beams. "And you saved the ship."

"It was a team effort." I unhook my helmet, lift it from my head and smile back. "What happened out there? I thought I saw something hit you."

Falling for Alice

"It was some more space debris," he says with a shake of his head. "We always know it's a threat, but I never thought it would actually happen. Fourteen times I've been on a spacewalk, and not once has anything gone wrong. Not once has *any* astronaut been hit by debris. I'm not thrilled to be the first."

"At least you'll go down in the history books," I say with a grin. Because even though things could have gone horribly wrong, he is alive, I am alive, the ship is okay, and I cannot stop my lips from spreading across my face. I wish my dad could see me now.

"And so will you, Alice. The girl who saved Wonder."

Glancing around the space station, it's hard to see it now as the place where I've struggled so hard to survive. "I think it's the other way around actually. Wonder saved me."

- THE END -

Vine Leaves Press Books

Cellography
by Christine Tsen

We All Reach The Earth By Falling
by Bauke Kamstra

Harvest
by Amanya Maloba

The Best of Vine Leaves Literary Journal 2014
edited by Jessica Bell

The Best of Vine Leaves Literary Journal 2013
edited by Jessica Bell and Dawn Ius

The Best of Vine Leaves Literary Journal 2012
edited by Jessica Bell and Dawn Ius

Polish Your Fiction: A Quick & Easy Self-Editing Guide
by Jessica Bell

Writing in a Nutshell: Writing Workshops to Improve Your Craft, by Jessica Bell

Indiestructible: Inspiring Stories from the Publishing Jungle
compiled and edited by Jessica Bell

Forthcoming titles

Solace
by Colleen Mills (June 15, 2015)

Self-Publish Your Book: A Quick & Easy Step-By-Step Guide
by Jessica Bell (2015)

Lightning Source UK Ltd.
Milton Keynes UK
UKHW04f0625130918
328823UK00001B/58/P